CATCH A MOONBEAM

After the death of her father, Melanie Jordan decides to give up her career as a musician to run the family business. She is persuaded to accompany her father's friend and her nephew, the conductor Carlton Kendall, whose arm has been injured in an accident. Marcia Dawson the soprano also joins the party, but soon Melanie suspects that there is a mystery behind the accident and questions the true value of the old violin which her father left.

MARY JANE WARMINGTON

CATCH A MOONBEAM

Complete and Unabridged

LINFORD
Leicester

First published in Great Britain in 1980

First Linford Edition
published 2006

British Library CIP Data

Warmington, Mary Jane
    Catch a moonbeam.—Large print ed.—
Linford romance library
    1. Love stories
    2. Large type books
    I. Title
823.9'14 [F]

ISBN 1–84617–185–7

Published by
F. A. Thorpe (Publishing)
Anstey, Leicestershire

Set by Words & Graphics Ltd.
Anstey, Leicestershire
Printed and bound in Great Britain by
T. J. International Ltd., Padstow, Cornwall

This book is printed on acid-free paper

1

Melanie Jordan strapped down her largest trunk, and sat back on her heels. This could have been the most exciting day of her life but for the sadness of losing her father only a month before. Alexander Jordan had always been so full of health and vigour, but a bout of virus pneumonia had accelerated a heart condition, and Melanie could hardly believe that he had gone.

Slowly she moved over to the window, looking down on the busy streets of Barholme. She had been born in this flat above the well-established music shop which Alexander Jordan had built up over the years. Her mother had helped him to keep the books, and when she died two years ago, Melanie had come home from Music College to take her place. She had studied piano and violin, gaining a degree in both, but regretfully she acknowledged to herself that she was unlikely to become famous with either of them.

'I haven't got the spark,' she had told her father. 'I'm competent, I guess, but that's all. I might as well stay at home and take Mother's place.'

'Not until you are absolutely sure,' Mr. Jordan told her, firmly. 'I can do the books, and young George Aldridge from next door can help in the shop. He would much rather be working in a music shop than a hardware store. His father can manage quite well without him at the moment.'

Melanie bit her lip. George Aldridge had been her constant companion while they were growing up, George being two years older than she. Melanie knew he was in love with her, and hoped to marry her one day. But when she thought of a future with George and herself managing the music shop, while she gave lessons to the local children, Melanie often felt trapped, and frustrated. Surely there was more to life than a safe haven in the small Border town of Barholme, even though she loved it beyond measure.

Melanie had finished her training and was able to write L.R.A.M. after her name, but before she could settle down, she was numbed by the shock of finding herself on her own. The Aldridges had been wonderful, especially George, who seemed to take it for granted that they would marry after a decent interval, and he would carry on managing Jordan's.

'You know I love you, Melanie,' he told her, a few days after the funeral. 'I've always known we would marry one day.'

'Please . . . no, George. I . . . I don't want to marry . . . anyone.'

'It's natural to feel like that,' said George, comfortably. He was a stocky young man with pleasant features and an air of satisfaction borne out of having been treated kindly by the world. George had never been truly disappointed in his whole life. Now he would not take 'No' for an answer.

'We'll leave it for a few months, Melanie,' he told her, 'until you begin to feel more . . . er . . . more normal. Meanwhile, I'll just carry on in the shop . . . that is, if you *wish* me to . . .'

'Of course, George,' she said, almost mechanically. 'I'll be glad of your help.'

When she felt a little better, Melanie had gone over her father's accounts, realising that her mother had had the true business sense in the firm. Alexander Jordan's great hobby had been violin-making, which he supposedly did in his spare time, but Melanie was slowly realising that he had spent more time on his violins than on running the business. He had sold the violins for a fraction of the cost of making them, and now she would have to consider her future very carefully. She might manage to avoid a few rocks which lay ahead, but if not, the business might have to be sold.

Melanie had not discussed her fears with George. She felt a strange

4

reluctance to confide in him too deeply. After a few days during which she had the heart-breaking task of sorting out her father's personal papers, Melanie decided she would help George in the shop during the mornings, and teach music in the afternoons. Most of her prospective pupils were probably at school. Her plans did not exactly fill her with delight, but she reminded herself that she was lucky to have Jordan's, and a comfortable flat to live in.

Two Sundays ago Melanie had excused herself from having another long discussion with George about her future. A few large bills had come in and she had to review her position, finding that it was easier for her to concentrate when she was on her own.

She had been adding up columns of figures with the aid of a pocket calculator when she heard a car drawing up in the side street below her window. A few moments later the house bell rang shrilly.

Melanie put down the calculator

reluctantly, her head still buzzing with her efforts to make sense of her finances, and ran lightly downstairs to open the door which she had shut for privacy. A tall, rather imposing-looking woman stood on the doorstep.

'Hello, Melanie, my dear,' she said. 'How are you?'

'Miss Kendall! How . . . how very nice to see you. I . . . ah . . .'

'May I come in, child? I'm sorry I haven't called on you before, but I've been out of the country. Shut the door like a good girl, and we'll go up and talk. Don't worry . . . I know the way. I've known your parents well enough over the years so that we needn't stand on ceremony'.

'Yes, of course,' said Melanie.

Miss Kendall was a member of a well-known family whose sole interest was music, and she had often come to see Mr. Jordan to discuss violins, both old and new. Alexander Jordan had often been able to restore old instruments for Miss Kendall and other

6

well-known musicians known to her. Her brother had been a well-known cellist, and her nephew, Carlton Kendall, even better known because of television. He was one of the youngest orchestral conductors in Britain, though recently he had met with an accident to his right arm. Melanie's own troubles had prevented her from taking more interest in the details of this accident, though she had read about it with strangely mixed feelings. She had met him only once under very difficult circumstances, and had decided that of all people she had ever met he was the most insufferable, yet Carlton Kendall had that extra something which made him an outstanding violinist. An injured arm would be more than usually tragic for him.

Melanie shut the door and followed Miss Kendall upstairs to her comfortable lounge. Fortunately she had lit a fire since the breezes had a cold bite to them. Miss Kendall had removed her hat and gloves, and now she plumped herself down on the chesterfield.

7

'Would you care for tea?' Melanie asked.

'Later, my dear. Just pour me a glass of dry sherry, or perhaps Madeira would do. Have one yourself, too.'

'Thank you,' said Melanie, rather weakly.

'I'd have come earlier, if I'd known. It . . . it was a big shock to me, hearing about Alex . . . a very big shock. I'm so sorry, Melanie, so sorry. It . . . it was a shock . . . yes . . .'

Miss Kendall removed a large handkerchief from her handbag and wiped her eyes, then blew her nose.

'I . . . I loved your father, you know, my dear. *And* your mother. I admired her very much. When we were young . . . Alex and I . . . I tried very hard to gain his love. In fact, I worked myself to a standstill to make him notice me. Then Betty Moryson came along one day and walked off with Alex without any effort at all. He fell in love with her, you see. It was as simple as that. And now they've both gone, poor darlings, and only you are left. I've come to do my best for you, child, because knowing Alex, he'll have left things in a muddle. Betty had the brains and Alex the talent. You might be a lucky girl, and have both!'

Melanie sat down. She had always faded into the background when Miss Kendall arrived, and in recent years she had seen little of the older lady, but now Melanie was receiving all her attention as Miss Kendall eyed her intently.

'What are you going to do with your life?' she asked, accepting a shortbread biscuit.

'I've been keeping the business going, with the help of George Aldridge from next door . . .'

'Nice young man, but he's inclined to be dull, dear.'

' . . . and I thought I'd try to find some pupils and teach.'

'Ah yes. Now, let me see . . . was it the piano, or the violin?'

'Both,' said Melanie, 'though I think

9

that was a mistake. But Father loved the violin, and Mother the piano. I think they wanted to express that love through me. At any rate, I've studied both, but I'm really only competent, Miss Kendall. I've known for . . . for a little time, that I'm no concert artist.'

'Wise child, if you *really* can assess your own limitations. So many struggle on to eventual disappointment refusing to accept the obvious. So you want to teach . . . '

'I don't *want* to. I think I'll *have* to.'

'Ah, so Alex *has* left his affairs in a mess. I thought so.'

Melanie's face coloured.

'I didn't say that, Miss Kendall,' she said, stiffly. 'I'll soon pull the business straight again. I only said . . . '

Millicent Kendall smiled. 'I'm sorry, my dear, I do rattle on. It's just that I like to get a true picture, not an idealized one. Your assessment of your own gifts encouraged me to think you felt the same way. You can make quite a good life for yourself here, but you're young and you're afraid it's going to be dull. Am I right?'

Melanie stared. In spite of herself, she laughed a little. Miss Kendall was inclined to bulldoze herself through to the core of the matter, but she was very shrewd.

'Absolutely right.'

'Pour yourself another sherry, dear. You look as though you need it. Couldn't you put in a good manager for a few months, and take a job away from home? We could get someone trustworthy. George is a nice boy, but he has no imagination. He'll sell what is on the shelves, book in the money, tidy up and do the dusting, and he'll think he has done a fine day's work. But he'll never have the inspiration to re-stock with new, imaginative goods which are not too absurd to appeal to people in Barholme. He won't move with the times. No, you'll need to employ someone else . . .'

'I shan't be able to afford it,' said Melanie, firmly.

'We'll go into that later. At the moment we're discussing whether or not you'd be willing to leave here for a month or two. It would do you good to get away.'

Melanie sighed. It *would* be wonderful to get away, but Miss Kendall surely had no real idea of her situation. She had to think twice before taking a bus trip to Edinburgh!

'I'd love to get away, but . . .'

'Then that's settled,' said Miss Kendall, with satisfaction, 'you're the very girl for the job.'

'What job?'

'You can write down music to dictation, I presume?'

'Yes.'

'Splendid. I told Carlton I could find him the right girl. He wishes to go away for a short while on holiday. I shall arrange it for him, and Bert Sloan will go along to take care of him . . . that's the man who is looking after him while his arm is so disabling . . . a very competent man, most trustworthy.

12

Carlton is not interested in arranging anything, so I have decided on Greece. A cruise, perhaps ... yes ... that would stir the imagination, if I can arrange it ... '

Melanie was becoming confused. She was not at all sure what sort of job was being offered, but in any case, it was completely out of the question. She could never accept a job where she was likely to be in contact with Carlton Kendall, nor was he likely to employ her. Though, of course, he may not remember the young student who tended to speak her mind.

He had been asked to conduct a Young People's Orchestra, to encourage the students at College, and three students had been sent along to audition for the Grieg Piano Concerto. Melanie had been one of them.

But unfortunately, they had not found Mr. Kendall in the best of humours, and after he had listened to one of the other students, and been called away briefly, had come storming back to announce that he could not audition anyone else that day.

Melanie had found it difficult to scrape together her expenses for the special journey, and she remembered the hard work and the hours of practice which had gone into making her note-perfect. The quick temper which went with her dark red hair came to the fore and she stood up.

'It isn't fair!' she cried. 'Perhaps you are busy, but it hasn't been easy for us either. It wouldn't hurt you to spare us a few more minutes of your time . . . '

There had been an awful silence while one of the other girls muttered angry remarks under her breath, swearing that Melanie had fouled things up for them. Carlton Kendall had paused, then nodded grimly, saying he would hear all three, but Melanie's fingers had been all thumbs. She was one of the two who failed, and she had to admit, miserably, that it was because she just wasn't good enough. She had caught a gleam in Mr. Kendall's eyes, and she wanted to shout at him to stop looking so smug.

She had faded into the background, playing one of the second violins in the Young People's Orchestra at the concert later in the month. It had been a big success, but she had hated the polished way Mr. Kendall took the applause, smiling with his usual charm. Melanie had wondered what his public would think of him if they had seen the superior young man she saw at rehearsals. He certainly was not her favourite person!

And now his Aunt Millicent wanted her to take on a job working for Mr. Kendall . . . on some sort of cruise round the Greek Islands? Surely she could not have heard aright.

'I . . . I don't understand . . . ' she began.

'Perfectly simple,' said Miss Kendall. 'You can go along with Carlton and Sloan. Carlton can neither play nor conduct at the moment, but he feels the

15

need for an outlet, so I've suggested that he tries his hand at composing. He's done quite a lot of it in the past, but now he must do it seriously. He needs inspiration, however, and he can't go *too* far away, nor must he face a climate which is too cold or wet. He has always loved the Greek influence in music, so I shall arrange for him to go to Greece. It had better be an arranged holiday, since he is in no mood to decide things for himself, nor would I put that responsibility on to a young girl like you. No, all three of you will do very well together. You will take along manuscript, and Carlton can dictate to you, and you can write it down. He cannot write at the moment. Besides, if he knows you are there each day, waiting for dictation, then it will encourage him to work, and not to back-slide . . .'

'But . . . but I don't think he'll *want* me,' put in Melanie, hurriedly. 'I auditioned with him once, but . . .'

'He had some scathing things to say.'

'More or less.'

'I'm not asking you to play soothing music each evening to get him off to sleep. I'm only asking you to copy down the music which he will be composing. It will be orchestrated later, so don't worry on that account. This is quite a different thing. Well, child, where's your coat?'

'My coat?'

'Yes, it's chilly at this time of year. I'll take you to Ardlui, Carlton's home in Edinburgh, and we can discuss terms. Will that make you feel better? I've also got someone in mind for your shop. Jane Price and her daughter, Shelley. Jane needs temporary accommodation, as she and Shelley have just returned from abroad. Andrew Price was in the Army, you know, and they all lived in Germany, but Andrew met with a sad accident and died, so Jane has brought young Shelley home. They're staying with me for the moment. They could live here, in your flat, and run the business for you. Jane was a competent business woman before she married Andrew . . . '

Melanie's head was reeling again. She remembered her father once calling Miss Kendall a 'managing woman'. It was the nearest he had come to criticizing anyone. With an inward smile, Melanie thought she knew why Miss Kendall had not got very far with her shy and rather awkward father.

She was suddenly aware of a footstep on the stairs, and there was a quick knock on the door of the lounge. Melanie frowned. Surely she had shut the door downstairs.

Going over she was about to open the door when it swung inwards, and George Aldridge peered round the door.

'George! How did you get in?' asked Melanie, who had been feeling rather startled.

'Your father gave me a key,' he said, holding it up. 'It was easier while he didn't feel so well. I . . . I just thought I heard . . . Oh, hello, Miss Kendall. I rather wondered if it was your car up the side street.'

George looked very much at home and Melanie coloured as she caught sight of Miss Kendall's raised eyebrows. How was she interpreting her friendship with George! He should not be breaking in on a private visit.

'We're talking business, young man,' said Miss Kendall.

'Oh, well then perhaps I have a personal interest,' said George. 'I'm Melanie's assistant, you know.'

'As soon as it affects you, I'll let you know, George,' said Melanie, feeling ruffled, 'and in the meantime . . . ' She turned uncertainly to Miss Kendall, 'I have to go to Edinburgh.'

'Why Edinburgh?' asked George.

Melanie's cheeks grew hot again. George's air was very proprietary.

'It's rather personal, George,' she explained, quietly. 'It hasn't got a direct bearing on the shop.'

Miss Kendall was rising.

'And now, if you'll get your coat, my

dear, I'd just like to make a telephone call. It's been so nice to see you again, George dear,' she said, turning to him. 'Goodbye for now.'

George found himself propelled towards the top of the stairs.

'He's not a very sensitive young man,' said Miss Kendall. 'I've had to argue with George before. Now, dear, I'll just ring up Carlton to make sure he's free, and hasn't got that Marcia with him.'

There was no need to ask who 'that Marcia' was, thought Melanie. There was only one Marcia Dawson, the world famous mezzo-soprano. Her recordings, with the Caledonian Orchestra conducted by Carlton Kendall, were famous and rumour had it that she and the young conductor were planning marriage. Melanie felt rather sorry for her on that account.

She turned away as Miss Kendall picked up the phone, and began a somewhat incomprehensible argument with her nephew.

'You said Marcia would not go with you because of an American engagement, and you need to get away, Carl . . . No, I don't want you just wandering off anywhere. This way everything will be organized for you . . . Yes, Melanie Jordan is very competent. I'm bringing her to see you now, dear . . . Oh . . . Oh? . . . Well, it can't be helped. Of course I can vouch for her . . . I was almost her mother, you know. She's Alex's daughter . . . you remember Alex, of course . . . Very well, I'll discuss salary and let her know where to join us in London . . . I presume we'll be at the hotel . . . very well, dear, I'll see to it . . . '

Miss Kendall put down the telephone, and sat staring into space for some time, then she sighed deeply and rose to her feet.

'You won't need your coat, Melanie. Carlton can't see you at the moment, and besides, he thinks it is unnecessary. He thinks it is enough that I can vouch for you.'

21

'But it isn't!' Melanie protested. 'And to be quite honest, Miss Kendall, I don't think I ought to accept the job.'

'Not accept it! But it's only for a few weeks. One week, perhaps, or less in London, then a holiday in Greece and the Greek Islands, then back to London, or Edinburgh. It will do you all the good in the world. By that time, I shall have fixed Jane Price up with a home of her own since she is completely out of touch with things after Germany, and you can either settle down here and run Jordan's yourself, or see more clearly the best way to arrange things. If you get very hard up, then I have an idea about that too, but just handing it all over to that young man, the Aldridge boy, is no solution.'

It sounded wonderful, thought Melanie, reluctantly. It was just what she needed, to get away and think about her future.

'I . . . I still think he won't want me because of that other time. I . . . I was rather rude . . . '

'Splendid! So you can stand up to him. Though my guess is that he'll have forgotten he has ever met you before. Carlton is bad at remembering people.'

Melanie felt rather deflated. Was she such a non-entity that people forgot who she was in a matter of weeks? Yet, in a way, that was rather comforting. She could fade into the background, and take Mr. Kendall's dictation when he felt the mood on him. Thank goodness she had perfect pitch! After work, she would no doubt be free to enjoy the sights. It was like some wonderful dream come true, she thought, remembering how often she had wanted to travel. Apart from one or two visits to France, she had not been out of the country.

'That Marcia seems to be making difficulties of some kind,' Miss Kendall went on, musingly. 'Why Carl doesn't show her the door, I can't imagine. Ah well . . . '

She began to discuss salary, waving

away Melanie's protests that she was being too well paid, with a holiday thrown in.

'You'll earn it,' Miss Kendall said, drily, 'with Carlton in his present mood. His accident was . . . was rather hard for him to bear . . .'

'What caused it?' asked Melanie, curiously.

'Perhaps he'll tell you one day. If you don't know, you can't sympathize, and he hates sympathy. I'll let you know when to arrive in London. We'll be staying at a hotel in Kensington where Carlton always stays . . . quiet but comfortable. But come prepared to travel as you'll only be a short time in London. There's a good girl. Oh my, but you do look like your dear father at times. He had just that colour of dark chestnut hair and green eyes. It was all wasted on a man, so make the most of it, dear. And don't let young George bully you. He's a bulldozer, if I remember rightly.'

'But I might be in love with him,

Miss Kendall,' said Melanie, her eyes twinkling. Her private thoughts were that Miss Kendall was rather a bulldozer herself!

Miss Kendall paused on her way to the door.

'Are you?' she asked, with interest.

'No.'

'I thought not. Not your type at all. 'Voir, my dear. I'll be in touch soon and I'll send Jane and Shelley to see you. Can you manage till then?'

'Perfectly,' said Melanie. 'Goodbye, Miss Kendall.'

After the older woman had clattered downstairs and driven off with a great deal of noise and engine revving, Melanie sat down, exhausted. Yet in spite of her exhaustion, she felt more alive than she had done since her father died. She was going to have to tell George about Mrs. Price, and her daughter, and George was not going to like it at all.

Yet Miss Kendall had cleared her mind of cobwebs where George was concerned. He really was the wrong person to be in charge of Jordan's. It was one thing to help out on a Saturday when the shop was busy, and quite another to run the place. Perhaps Mrs. Price would be a big help with regard to this.

But Miss Kendall must surely be the most managing woman Melanie had ever met! And she certainly believed in killing several birds with one stone. She was sending her nephew on a cruise, encouraging his interest in composing by having Melanie at his elbow to take down his dictation, and fixing up her friend with a temporary home in Melanie's flat.

But nothing is perfect, Melanie remembered. She and Carlton Kendall were not at all compatible. She was going to need all her energy to stand up to George, and perhaps Mrs. Price would hate the sight of the place.

The doorbell shrilled, and Melanie went back downstairs, to find George on the doorstep once more.

'So you didn't go with that awful woman,' he said, with satisfaction. 'I can't stand Miss Kendall. Look, Melanie, there are things we must discuss.'

'Not now, George, I'm tired.'

'Tomorrow then.'

'Tomorrow,' she agreed.

'Nine o'clock sharp?'

'Okay.'

She shut the door, thinking that George must have been hovering around so that he could watch Miss Kendall leaving without her. Annoyance brought a renewal of energy. She was certainly going to have to argue things out with George. Had she really encouraged him so much? she wondered, her cheeks hot. Perhaps, by being weak, she had allowed him to think that she would marry him one day, and that Jordan's was practically his!

But no, she had not! thought Melanie, after a great deal of consideration. He had never listened to her protests. But he would have to listen now.

2

The interview with George was worse than anything she could have imagined, thought Melanie. In the quiet of the night she was remembering that he had helped quite a lot while her father was alive, and she knew she was going to be accused of ingratitude to say the least. Disappointment brought out a few more adjectives from George, and he made a convincing case, so that Melanie felt as low as they come.

'I know you've been a tower of strength, George,' she assured him.

'Only until Miss Kendall comes along and offers you something better,' he declared, bitterly. 'Who is this Mrs. Price? You're actually stupid enough to employ her as manageress on Miss Kendall's say-so, without even meeting her! And you take a temporary job, when the quicker you get going with finding a few pupils, the better. You aren't exactly the heiress to millions . . . '

'That's enough, George,' said Melanie, flushing at his sneers. 'It's still *my* shop, and I will run it as I like. If I choose to take a job, that's my affair. And if I want two ladies to stay in my flat and work in my shop while I'm away, then I shall arrange it without asking your permission. Now, if you enjoy helping, I'm sure Mrs. Price will be pleased to have you, but I'm not handing it all over to you . . . '

'You were until That Woman arrived,' George yelled. 'You even fancied me.'

'I've never fancied you,' said Melanie. 'I can't marry you, George. I don't love you.'

They were yelling at one another, in the shop, and suddenly Melanie noticed one or two interested customers listening avidly. It would be all over Barholme in no time, she thought. It was a good job she *was* going away.

'Melanie . . . '

'We can't talk now, George,' she said, more quietly. 'We've got someone waiting. I'll see to it.'

'We can't leave things like this,' he said. 'You're upset. You aren't thinking straight. Look, we'll leave it for now, and we can discuss it all when you've got over things a little.'

She didn't answer. She took the money for an L.P. someone had chosen, and found a mouth organ for a small boy's birthday gift. Suddenly she was missing her father very much indeed, and wanted to run away and cry her heart out.

But there was a great deal of work still to be done before Mrs. Price arrived. She must leave her business affairs in good order, and she must know how much she could pay for help of this kind. Doggedly Melanie worked on. If she got through the next few weeks, she must surely be able to weather any future blows which Fate might have in store.

But even as she thought about it,

Melanie shivered. Perhaps her troubles were only beginning!

★ ★ ★

Early on Sunday morning Miss Kendall telephoned to say that she would bring Mrs. Price and Shelley to meet Melanie that afternoon, and not to worry about cakes for tea because she would bring a chocolate sponge.

Melanie did not care for chocolate sponge, and she could have wished for a more convenient day. It had not been an easy week with George alternately in the huff, then full of persuasion for her to forget all about Miss Kendall and her offer of employment, and for them to make a go of Jordan's together. At times Melanie had weakened, wondering if this was the substance, while she was chasing the shadow. Ought she to settle for what she had? Why, if she started some new strange venture, she might end up in a financial mess, and there would not be enough in the sale of the business to put her straight again. She could very well end up destitute.

Then she would go for a walk, following a path to the river which briefly touched the outskirts of Barholme. There, in the soft soothing lull of rippling water, she would look at the dancing sunlight, made even brighter by the song of the birds, and wonder if the easy way was not the right one. Life beckoned, and something in her responded. How dull it would be, married to George, trying to teach when she had no real vocation for it, and hoping to make enough sales in the shop to pay the bills. George had never even brought her along the river walk, or tried to kiss her under the beautiful chestnut tree near the bend in the river.

Melanie had been at her weakest, however, when Miss Kendall telephoned, and she spent the morning tidying the flat, and polishing the shop counters, also baking scones and pancakes in case anyone else did not like sponge.

Mrs. Price proved to be a small slender woman in her late forties, with well-cut brown hair, and smiling eyes behind gold-rimmed spectacles.

Shelley looked very young and pretty, with fluffy fair hair, and blue eyes. She smiled at Melanie shyly, when Miss Kendall introduced them, having once again parked her car on the side street. No doubt George would be peering at them from the flat above the shop next door, thought Melanie. She would be glad when things were settled, one way or another.

'The flat is quite comfortable,' she said, showing Mrs. Price around. 'Mother was a born homemaker, though I'm afraid I haven't altered anything very much, apart from putting up new curtains and making new cushion covers. It could be rather dated now.'

'It's charming,' said Mrs. Price.

'Well . . . it's only for a short time,' said Melanie.

'It will seem like a lovely holiday for

Shelley and me. Things have been a bit . . . ah . . . upset . . . since Edward died. We need to find a new permanent home.'

'We'll find it for you,' said Miss Kendall. 'Don't worry yourself, Jane. We won't leave you in the lurch.'

Mrs. Price nodded and smiled a little, but Melanie could see the worry in her eyes, and she experienced a sudden fellow feeling. Mrs. Price would probably prefer to work out her own salvation, and that might not run parallel with Miss Kendall's ideas.

'Would you like tea first, or should we go down and look round the shop?' Melanie asked.

'Shop first, tea afterwards, then you can discuss it all over tea,' said Miss Kendall. 'Come along, Shelley dear. I expect all Melanie's sales of pop records will go sky-high when the local boys have a look at you. Not that Melanie isn't a draw . . . you're pretty enough, too, dear and in fact, you're well . . . ah . . . but Shelley . . . ah . . . '

'Is a knock-out?' asked Melanie, helpfully, her eyes dancing as she looked at the girl. Shelley blushed and smiled at her in return.

'Have you done this sort of thing before?' Melanie asked.

'No, I've been at school. I'm afraid I'm not really clever enough for a career.'

'She'll marry, won't she Jane?' asked Miss Kendall.

Again Melanie caught a worried look in Mrs. Price's eyes. No doubt she was concerned for Shelley's future. Melanie resolved to try and help her as best she could.

'It isn't a very big shop,' she said, as she showed them round, 'but there again, it's quite well laid out. If you decide you'd like to come, I shall show you where to find everything, and who to contact if you run out of stock, though you'll likely find plenty of travellers calling. There is a small workshop there, in the back of the shop, where Father pursued his great hobby, though I've never been very sure whether he was a violin-maker who decided to run a music business, or whether it was the other way round. At any rate, he made quite a few violins and violas. I have one he made specially for me, and there is another one which he made just before he died.'

'Splendid instruments,' said Miss Kendall. 'I recommended Alexander to a great many artists. He also restored old instruments . . . isn't that so, Melanie?'

'Yes, indeed he did. Sometime, I suppose, I'll have to sort through all this, but not just yet. I . . .'

She looked at Mrs. Price, and there was sympathy between them.

'Do you think you and Shelley would be able to cope?' she asked. 'I understand that I'll only be away a few weeks, but things aren't too good at the moment, and even a few weeks might mean disaster. George Aldridge helps on a Saturday, and was willing to come full time. He lives next door, by the way. I . . . I would introduce him to you, if you decide to stay.'

'I would find it an exciting challenge,' said Mrs. Price. 'You'll want to know my qualifications, too, you know . . .'

'And we would have to discuss terms,' went on Melanie.

'Let's go back upstairs and eat my chocolate sponge,' said Miss Kendall, beaming. It was obvious that Jane and young Melanie had taken to one another. She was always thoroughly satisfied when her schemes worked out.

The only fly in the ointment, as far as she could see, was the boy, George. Yes, indeed, the boy might prove a complication.

Melanie settled the terms with Mrs. Price very happily, delighted that things were going so well when she and the older woman had worked it all out. Miss Kendall asked her to travel to London the following Thursday, and a room would be arranged for her at the hotel. Mrs. Price and Shelley could not come until Friday, but Melanie gave them a key, and was assured that all would be well.

Miss Kendall had produced a substantial cheque, which she assured Melanie was from the sale of a viola her father had made, and she spent a wildly exciting day augmenting her wardrobe, and having her hair nicely cut. It was her best feature, and easy to manage, and it glowed with colour after a good shampoo and set.

Somehow she had managed to put Carlton Kendall completely out of her mind. He was merely a shadowy figure in the background.

It was only when she strapped down her luggage, and labelled it with the address of the London hotel, that Melanie came down to earth with a bump. Whatever had possessed her to go mad like this? She had a horrid vision of walking into the hotel, then having to turn tail and walk straight back out, after Carlton Kendall had taken one good look at her. How humiliating that would be! She had already been humiliated by him!

Nor could she come running home to Jordan's, having given up her flat to Mrs. Price and Shelley! She would have nowhere to go, and precious little money left for a hotel, if everything went wrong. Nor was Miss Kendall likely to help her, since she was sure to side with her nephew, if it came to a showdown.

Melanie swallowed her nervous fears, and took a grip on herself. There was no going back now. The taxi would be here in another few minutes, and on impulse she decided to go next door and have a word with George. She had asked him to call in and meet Mrs. Price on her last visit, and he had declined, huffily, then changed his mind. Melanie had a sneaking suspicion that he'd had an eyeful of Shelley from behind the frilled terylene curtains.

'I still think you're being a fool, Melanie,' he declared.

'You could be right, George,' she agreed. 'Look, don't let's quarrel. We've been neighbours since we were children. Mrs. Price and Shelley might need some help. Please be nice to them.'

'Yes, she looks a delicate little thing,' George nodded thoughtfully.

'They need the job, too. Mrs. Price lost her husband. He was in the Army, you know. They have to find a new home, so it's going to help a great deal if they stay here for a few weeks.'

'I see,' said George, mollified. 'Okay, don't worry, Melanie, I'll keep an eye on it all for you, if you've really made up your mind. Have a good time.'

'I'm going to work, George.'

'On a cruise?'

'Yes, on a cruise. Look, George, we've been through all this before, so don't let's quarrel again. 'Bye for now and . . . and I'll see you when I get back.'

Suddenly he pulled her into his arms, pinioning her own while he kissed her, almost bruising her mouth while she struggled to be free.

'I wish you hadn't done that, George.'

'And I wish I'd done it a lot more often. Look, Melanie, where can I find you? . . in case of emergency, I mean.'

She hesitated, then reluctantly gave him the address of the hotel in London, and the details of the cruise to the Greek Islands. As added incentive, Miss Kendall had primed her well regarding its attractions.

Melanie returned to the flat for her final clearing up. She had put her two most precious possessions . . . the old violin which had been in their family for generations and which her father had lovingly cared for, and the new which he had made himself, into a cupboard in her bedroom and locked the door. It wasn't that she did not trust Mrs. Price, but she felt that the instruments needed special care. She also locked private papers into a drawer of her desk, but apart from that, Mrs. Price and Shelley had access to everything. Melanie decided, thoughtfully, that she would leave the keys at her bank.

A moment later the taxi drew up at the side door and she climbed into it. There was no time for further thought, as her luggage was bundled into the taxi.

As she looked back, she could see George, a lonely figure, standing outside Jordan's.

Miss Kendall met Melanie at Euston Station. She had a taxi waiting, and Melanie was glad of the older woman's chatter as they drove out towards Kensington.

'I'm so glad you had a pleasant journey, dear, and that you're a good traveller. That's important because of the task which lies ahead. I want you to enjoy yourself, too, Melanie. How were Jane and Shelley? Have they settled in?'

'I think so,' Melanie agreed.

It all felt rather unreal, she thought, as she looked out on the busy London streets. They reached the charming hotel much quicker than she had anticipated, and Miss Kendall had her luggage taken up to her room, then escorted her to Carlton's sitting room on the second floor.

'This is Carlton,' she introduced, 'I think you've met Melanie before, Carl . . . Melanie Jordan . . . and here is Miss Marcia Dawson. You'll soon get to know one another.'

Carlton Kendall's eyes flickered for a moment, then he stared at Melanie without recognition. There was an air of tension about the place and for an awful moment she thought that her worst fears were going to be realized and she was about to be shown the door. Then she realized that the atmosphere had nothing to do with her. She wasn't important enough for that.

Miss Kendall was looking at Marcia Dawson apprehensively, and the cold stony look on Carlton Kendall's face was really controlled anger.

'I mean it, Carl, every word,' Marcia Dawson said, buttoning up the smart white wool cape which matched her suit exactly.

'I know you do.'

'Then you know where to find me, if you want me. Goodbye, Carl.'

She gave Melanie a brief look, then walked delicately to the door where she let herself out, quietly. Carlton Kendall stood staring at some papers spread out on a small table while Miss Kendall hovered about uncertainly.

'Er . . . shall I order tea, dear?' she asked. 'I'll show Melanie to her room, if you like, and I expect she wants tea . . .'

'Oh . . . whatever you like,' he told her, waving his hand.

Melanie hesitated. Mr. Kendall was supposed to be her employer, yet he had paid less attention to her than he would have done to a flea. What was there about this man which irritated her so much? she wondered. She tried to keep her temper, remembering the last time she had taken him to task, with disastrous results. Yet she had to know where she stood.

'Look, if I'm in the way,' she began. 'I

mean . . . if you really don't need me . . .'

He turned to stare at her again, and for the second time she thought there was a flicker of recognition in his eyes.

'I understand you've come to take down music at my dictation,' he said, quietly. 'At this moment I don't particularly feel like composing music, and I should imagine you don't particularly feel like setting it down in manuscript form, even if I did, after such a long journey. No? Well, go and have a wash, or have tea, and just . . . just take the evening off, or whatever Aunt Millicant has planned for you. I'm sure she's planned *something*.'

He paused and raised an eyebrow at his aunt who had nothing to say.

'Melanie and I could go out,' she said after a moment.

'If you don't mind, I'd rather like to rest this evening,' said Melanie, 'unless it's rather special. It was a long journey.'

'Of course, dear. It was only for your

entertainment. Have a wash, then we'll have tea. Will you have tea with us, Carl?'

'No, thank you, *I'm* going out,' said Mr. Kendall, and Melanie could see that he was still trembling with anger.

'Oh dear, but I rather think he's very upset,' said Miss Kendall, as he walked from the room.

'Has it anything to do with me?' asked Melanie.

'Of course not. You mustn't think such a thing.'

But Melanie was not at all sure whether or not to believe her.

'Miss Kendall, I really don't think . . .' she began, then stopped when she saw large tears welling up in the older woman's eyes.

'I'm a managing old woman,' she said, 'but I'm only concerned for Carl's happiness. You believe that, don't you, dear?'

'Yes, but . . .'

'Stay with me and do your best for him, and I'll do my best for you, Alex's daughter. Go to sleep now and be refreshed in the morning. We aren't due to leave Gatwick until Wednesday, so you can help me with some last minute shopping.'

'Of course, Miss Kendall.'

'I'm coming with you, my dear. I've decided it's essential. I can find the time, and I feel that this is a time in Carl's life when he needs all the help he can get. Bert Sloan will look after him and attend to the exercises he needs for his arm and that sort of thing, but you and I, dear, must attend to the real man. It's the real man who needs to be healed.'

Melanie nodded. In spite of herself, she had been rather shocked by Carlton Kendall's appearance, and she could not fail to see the signs of suffering on his face.

She would do her best for him, for his own sake as well as Miss Kendall's.

★ ★ ★

47

Next morning Bert Sloan arrived, and smiled pleasantly at Melanie. He was a thin man, in his forties, cheerful without being irritating.

'Miss Jordan is going to help Mr. Kendall with his music,' Miss Kendall explained.

'She'll cheer him up an' all, I reckon,' said Bert.

Melanie thought he was being hopeful. Mr. Kendall looked as though he was thoroughly enjoying his bad temper. She was glad to escape, with Miss Kendall, to her shopping spree. Melanie had only packed one swimsuit for herself, so Miss Kendall insisted in treating her to another, in pure white, with sandals to match.

'You won't be working all the time,' she said. 'Mop up the sun. And did you pack a cocktail dress? The Captain is sure to give a cocktail party, dear.'

'Yes, I packed one, just in case.'

'Good girl. I want you to look nice.'

Melanie began to look at Miss Kendall with slight suspicion. What had she in mind now? If she thought that Melanie was ever likely to get her dear Carl's 'mind off things' in any other way, apart from helping him with his music, then the idea was ludicrous! Melanie sighed, and began to wonder afresh if she had not been completely mad.

There was no time for further reflection, however. All too soon they were on their way to Gatwick Airport to catch the plane for Athens.

The previous evening Melanie had found herself alone with Mr. Kendall in the lounge of the hotel suite and for a time she had watched him prowling up and down like a caged animal, his face white and rather drawn. He paid no more attention to her than he did to the fly buzzing around the wallpaper.

Melanie had offered to work with him, taking his dictation to see whether Miss Kendall's ideas were practicable or not, but he had waved her away impatiently. Now she was remembering the tears in the older woman's eyes, and the temper which went with her dark chestnut hair began to bubble a little.

'Can't you stop feeling so sorry for yourself?' she asked, then felt appalled at her own temerity. The words seemed to re-echo round the room. Mr. Kendall had stopped in his tracks, then he swung round to stare at her.

'I beg your pardon.'

Melanie was about to apologize, then she changed her mind. She felt that the air had to be cleared and it was better to do so before they left London rather than having to endure this Greek holiday instead of enjoying the experience.

'I said wasn't it time you stopped feeling sorry for yourself? You're making Miss Kendall's life a misery, and mine too for that matter. If you don't want me, I'll go. If you don't want this holiday Miss Kendall has arranged for you, then say so, and look happy about it. But please don't crash about in a bad temper, or stand staring into corners in sulky silence. You're very hard to live with, and I'm very glad I'm only an employee and not a member of your family.'

'Then why don't you get out?' he flashed.

'Because a job is a job, and I need the money. My business isn't all that good at the moment.'

'But you don't want to do this job?'

'Not with you in such a mood. One could cut the atmosphere around here with a knife. If it weren't for that I would be enjoying every minute. I've never been to Greece. I've only been to France by Hovercraft, on a stormy day when I felt that my end had come. In spite of the uncertainty about whether or not I can earn my salary, I've been looking forward to this, but I don't fancy being around on sufferance, so if you want to fire me, please do it now. I deserve it for my impertinence to you and there's no real harm done at the moment. I can pay Miss Kendall back for all that she's lent me so far, though she swears it was from a violin sale.'

He was staring at her strangely.

'Oh yes . . . the violin sale. Your father was Alexander Jordan . . . and . . .'

'Yes, he died a short time ago,' she nodded. 'That's another reason why I wanted to get away.'

He had come to sit down near to her on a large easy chair, though she still felt that his thoughts were not entirely with her. Something else was troubling him.

'So I've been sulking?'

'Oh, I'm sorry, I shouldn't have said that, but . . . but you have been rather awful . . .'

This time she had his attention.

'And you've been a self-assured young female with accusing eyes and a way of tossing back your red hair to show you don't give a fig for me. You did that before at an audition, as I remember.'

She went scarlet. 'Oh dear . . . do you? I was afraid you might, but I didn't mean . . .'

'Didn't you? You set yourself up in

judgement on other people, yet you don't like it if they turn the tables. What about that old Indian proverb, that you must not judge a man until you have walked for seven days in his shoes. Perhaps we ought *both* to remember it.'

'Perhaps we . . . *I* should,' she agreed, in a small voice.

He was about to say more, but the door opened and Bert Sloan came in to ask about personal items for packing. Mr. Kendall had left most of them at his permanent home outside Edinburgh.

'If we need more items, then I can buy them in Athens,' he said. 'My wants are simple.'

Melanie saw the slight raising of Bert's eyebrows and deduced that her employer's wants were normally far from simple. She looked at him rather uneasily. It was difficult to tell how she stood now in his estimation, or whether or not she *had* cleared the air between them.

The telephone began to ring and he

picked up the receiver.

'It's for you,' he said, turning to her again and adding, 'your boy friend, George.'

'George!' Melanie's cheeks were like roses though her heart seemed to miss a beat. What had gone wrong now?

'What's wrong, George?' she asked anxiously.

'Someone's been wanting to contact you, about a violin, Melanie,' he told her.

'I'm afraid it will have to keep till I get back, George.'

'But it may be a good sale.'

'Than perhaps you could take particulars? A couple of weeks won't matter, if they are serious.'

'The other thing is . . . Shelley Price was asking about a key to a cupboard. She says it's locked.'

'I locked it, George,' Melanie told him. 'I think I mentioned it to Mrs. Price. It's got my personal things in there.'

Melanie paused, feeling disquieted.

Why did Shelley want to open a door which had obviously been locked for privacy?

'I miss you already, Mel,' George was saying.

Her voice softened. In these new surroundings, she missed George, too.

'I'll be back soon, George,' she promised and turned to find Carlton Kendall's brooding eyes on her again. He looked as withdrawn and sulky as ever, but Melanie could not have cared less. She was still thinking about the Prices when she went to bed. Just how much did she know about them? Mrs. Price had offered references, but Melanie had thought that Miss Kendall's word was enough. Now she was not so sure. Now she was wondering if she were wise to go so far away and leave her business in the hands of strangers.

3

Melanie had never flown before. There had never been enough money to go hopping around the world, and her trip to France had been by the shortest possible ferry route. Fortunately Miss Kendall had taken it for granted that she was a seasoned traveller, and Melanie had welcomed it that way. She did not want the fuss which the older lady might have made. She was a good sailor, but she found out the hard way that air travel was rather different. Her insides rebelled, and she sat miserably in her seat while Miss Kendall kept up a non-stop conversation.

Across the aisle, Carlton Kendall dozed while Bert Sloan sat beside him, apparently at ease with himself. Presently Miss Kendall rose to go along to the washroom, and Melanie felt she would have to make use of her small paper bag, but a moment later Mr. Kendall had slipped into the seat beside her.

'Feeling groggy?' he asked, kindly.

She nodded. 'This is my first flight,' she confessed.

'It's probably nerves then. I'll have the stewardess find you something. Just relax. Here, take my hand and you'll feel better.'

Melanie did not feel better as she lay back with her eyes closed. Miss Kendall had returned but she and Carlton seemed to have changed seats. He made Melanie drink something, and presently she began to feel more normal.

'Thank you,' she whispered.

His smile was like sunshine after thunder.

'Cheer up, your last day hasn't come,' he encouraged, and she managed a smile before he rose to his feet. He and Miss Kendall again swapped seats.

'Poor child, you should have told me,' she scolded.

Melanie said nothing, feeling embarrassed and ashamed that she had caused any fuss, though she did not relax completely until they finally touched down at Athens Airport, and she found herself being conducted towards a bus which took them on a twelve-mile journey to delightful cottages by the sea.

Melanie and Miss Kendall shared one of the cottages while Carlton and Bert Sloan were allocated another.

It was a lovely little cottage, thought Melanie when she had time to look round, with a kitchen, bedroom, sitting room and dining room. Though it was the bathroom which attracted Melanie, and Miss Kendall nodded kindly.

'Go ahead, child. Have your bath first, then get into bed. You'll feel better after a good sleep. We are here for two days, I understand, and you'll be able to do a bit of exploring tomorrow, and have a better look at Athens.'

'Oh, Miss Kendall, I *am* sorry to have been such a nuisance on the flight,' said Melanie, 'but I *am* a good sailor.'

'Then that's much more important,' the older woman told her. 'So is Carlton. That's when you'll be required to earn your holiday, my dear, so don't worry.'

Melanie was too tired to worry about anything, but she found herself remembering Carlton Kendall's kindness to her, just when she needed it most. He was a strange man, she thought, remembering that his smile was gentle and considerate when he thought she needed help, yet he could be just as unpleasant as, for example, when he called her to speak with George on the telephone. He hadn't looked at all pleased with her then!

Melanie remembered his eagerness when he went to pick up the receiver. Perhaps he had expected a call himself . . . from Marcia Dawson, perhaps? Was he upset and unhappy because of Miss Dawson?

Oh well, it was none of her business,

thought Melanie, yawning as she crawled into bed. She had thought she would be too excited to sleep, but she was wrong. In spite of the roar of jets overhead, and the beat of the sea about five yards away, Melanie slept . . . and slept . . .

★ ★ ★

It was Miss Kendall who woke her next morning after Carlton had knocked on their door. It was a lovely sunny morning and Melanie leapt out of bed feeling energetic and refreshed.

'Make some coffee, dear,' said Miss Kendall, and obediently Melanie went into the small kitchen, which was cool and fresh with stone floors and sliding doors. Outside the sun shone brilliantly and Melanie looked out a pale lemon sundress and matching sandals after she and Miss Kendall had refreshed themselves with the early morning coffee.

'We'll go along to the dining room for lunch,' Miss Kendall told her. 'We'd better all walk along together . . . along the sea wall. See what Carl is doing this morning though, dear. I expect he is just getting his bearings like the rest of us.'

It was a day which Melanie long remembered as one of the happiest she had known. Carlton Kendall looked years younger as he leaned against the sea wall, clad in an open-necked shirt and white slacks. A number of their party were milling about, and Bert Sloan was chatting to a man of his own age who was trying to control two excited school children while he waited for his wife to finish some chores.

'Even on holiday, she has to clean up,' he grinned.

Carlton turned and smiled lazily at Melanie and she was relieved that he did not refer to her poor flight.

'Miss Kendall says it would be nice if we all went along together to have lunch in the dining room,' she ventured.

'Only if she hurries up over her

make-up and doesn't spend too much time sticking on false eyelashes and combing out her wig,' he grinned.

Melanie laughed aloud. Apart from a surreptitious dab of powder, Miss Kendall showed a washed face to the world. She did not approve of too much make-up, even on young girls.

'How does this suit you, Melanie?' he asked.

Her heart suddenly beat faster. This was the first time he referred to her by her Christian name.

He was looking down as the sea lazily lapped against the wall. The air was like wine, and the sun shone with brilliance against a wonderfully clear blue sky. It all felt strangely unreal, yet solidly beautiful, so that she had no sense of living in a dream.

'It's . . . it's wonderful,' she said, softly. 'I feel as though I have stepped into a beautiful picture.'

'It gives one an appetite. I should have eaten more for breakfast after all. Perhaps Aunt Millicent knew what she was doing when she practically threw me into having this holiday.'

He turned and she noticed that his shirt had long sleeves and his right arm looked stiff and rigid. She longed to ask him what had happened, but she felt afraid of breaking his present mood. If only he were always like this, what a marvellous working holiday this could be!

A moment later Miss Kendall had joined them and they all began to take the lovely walk, along the sea wall, to the dining room where Melanie hoped to have her first taste of Greek food.

The dining room was charming, with white walls and flowers everywhere. Melanie had little idea as to what she was eating for lunch, but it tasted wonderful, especially after the walk with the sea air sharpening her appetite.

She tucked into her food, heartily, then paused to look at Carlton Kendall, realizing almost for the first time why Bert Sloan was so valuable to him. Because of his injured arm, the food had to be cut into small pieces, and this time there was no friendliness in his dark eyes as he met the sympathy in hers.

She flushed deeply, and her appetite dimished so that she pushed her plate away.

'Not eating, dear?' asked Miss Kendall.

'There . . . there's rather a lot,' said Melanie.

'It's the olive oil, and it's too rich for us,' said Miss Kendall, eating her own food with a great deal of enjoyment. 'There's a bus trip to Sounion this afternoon. Why don't you take Melanie, Carl, and Bert can help me with one or two small jobs.'

'I don't see why we can't all go,' said Carlton, smoothly. 'I'm sure Bert would be happy to help you, but he would also enjoy looking at the ancient Temple of Poseidon as much as any of us.'

'Oh yes, please let's all go, Miss Kendall,' said Melanie, hurriedly.

Whatever was the older woman

thinking about? she wondered. It was almost as though she were pushing her and Carlton Kendall together! Yet nothing could be more unsuitable. She had suspected once or twice that the older lady had some scheme in mind.

Melanie met Bert Sloan's amused eyes, and flushed as he smiled at her surreptitiously. Perhaps he had already been treated to a crop of Miss Kendall's 'arrangements'.

'Oh, very well,' Miss Kendall said, rather testily, 'though don't expect me to come every time. I'm an old woman now, you know.'

'I'll remind you about that next time you forget it,' Carlton laughed.

Greece was so different from anything she had ever seen, thought Melanie, as they drove along the coast road towards Glyfada and Vouliagmeni. If only her employer had not been in a mood again, how she would have enjoyed it! Yet she felt he had resented having been pushed into this holiday by his aunt, and having to put up with Melanie into the bargain, and sometimes, when he felt anti-social, he resented it. Her cheeks flushed at the thought of it, and her temper which was always there to plague her, began to bubble. Now it was her turn to be silent, and when they reached Sounion, and the party was conducted towards the very beautiful Temple of Poseidon, built in the 5th Century, B.C., Melanie was again caught between enchantment and depression.

'Well? Don't you find it fascinating?' asked Carlton, by her side.

'It's utterly beautiful, but . . . '

'But what? Have you got gyppy-tum again? You look as though you have.'

'And you look as though you'd rather be anywhere than enjoying this,' she said, the words tumbling out before she could stop them. Why couldn't she learn to hold her tongue!

Carlton turned round to look at her thoughtfully.

'I . . . I'm sorry,' she apologized. 'I'm

always putting my foot in it. But for a little while you seemed to be happy, then you looked so . . . so fed up back there in the dining room, and when Miss Kendall mentioned Sounion . . . '

'I love Sounion,' said Carlton. 'I'm just not used to going there in a bus, that's all. If it were not for this beastly arm, I could hire a car in Athens, though it would mean Bert having to drive. I hate having to do things by the clock, yet . . . in a way . . . it's good for me to travel like this, otherwise I *make* myself do everything. Are you afraid I might sit in a corner and . . . and sulk again?'

He was grinning at her, and she found herself responding. His ill humour had nothing to do with her after all. It was only because of his injured arm.

'I'm sorry. I feel a fool. I suppose you would sack me if we were in London, but it isn't so easy here, is it?'

'No, you'll be able to take me to task as often as you please. I'll just dock it off your salary.' He stared at her solemnly. 'You've got practically nothing to come!'

'I'm sorry,' she said again. 'I know it's a great fault, and Father used to try to put me right, and to teach me to curb my tongue. He said it would get me into trouble one day.'

'You miss him?'

She nodded. 'Yes. I'd like to think he is still keeping an eye on me, though, and is happy for me at the moment.'

He nodded and squeezed her fingers. He was really very attractive, she thought, with an inward thrill of excitement.

'Now we all get herded back into the bus,' said Carlton, 'so that we'll be back in Athens in time for dinner. According to my notes, we're off to the Plaka.'

Again he turned to smile at her.

'Never mind, let's enjoy it, Melanie. Tomorrow we go on board ship, then you will have to start work, and you'll be saying your piece more and more often because I shall work you to death.

Already I'm listening to the music of this place. I can hear it so loudly, it's a wonder you don't hear it with me.'

For a long moment they stood side by side, looking up at the ancient Temple, and again Melanie felt her senses stirring.

'I shall love doing the work with you,' she said, softly.

'Will you?'

He turned to her, his eyes alight, so that his whole body seemed to glow with an inward flame. In that moment Melanie knew there was nothing she would not do for Carlton Kendall.

He was still in a happy, joyous mood that evening as they gathered once again to drive to Athens. Melanie had changed into a gold-coloured cocktail dress with matching sandals, while Miss Kendall wore navy blue. Melanie's beautiful dark chestnut hair shone with brushing.

'They do us credit, don't they, Bert?' asked Carlton.

'They certainly do, Mr. Kendall,' said

Bert, grinning. He was only too happy to have his employer in a better mood.

Melanie found that the Plaka was a district of night life with narrow winding lanes and a great deal of noise, yet a strange madness seemed to grip her, and once again she found herself relishing her dinner.

'Do you like squids and octopus,' said Carlton, in her ear.

Melanie threw down her fork in horror, while he laughed with delight, his eyes mocking.

'The next outburst will cost you ten pounds,' he told her.

'You deserve it,' she said. 'I . . . I was just enjoying this food.'

'Then carry on enjoying it, for goodness sake. If you like it does it matter what it is?'

'Yes,' she said, emphatically.

'Funny child,' he told her. 'Never mind, have some wine, then everything will taste wonderful. Life will be wonderful, little Melanie.'

In so many ways, life was wonderful

already, thought Melanie as she sipped her wine. In spite of his teasing, Carlton Kendall made her feel more alive than anyone had ever done. For a moment she thought again about her father, and how much he would have enjoyed all this. Sometimes it really did seem that she could feel his presence near, and surely he must be happy to know she was enriching her life in this way.

'What are you thinking about?' Carlton asked her. 'You have the most expressive face, Melanie Jordan. It shows up all the sunshine and shadows of your mind.'

'Your face closes like a shut door at times,' she returned.

'You can't get away by throwing the ball to me,' he said. 'Are you missing the boy friend? George, isn't it?'

Melanie had almost forgotten George, but now she remembered him, and Mrs. Price, not to mention Shelley who wanted the key to a locked cupboard. Melanie's eyes grow grave again, and she said nothing so that Carlton turned away.

'I think we are about to be treated to some Greek dances and bouzouki music, though perhaps it can't compete with the night life in Barholme. Have some more retsina.'

'That will do, Carl,' Miss Kendall broke in, 'I don't want Melanie upset. It's time we got back to the cottage in any case. Don't worry, dear, you'll see more of Athens before we go home.'

Melanie looked at Carlton and wondered what sort of music he could 'hear' in Athens. No doubt it would be a series of crashing cords, full of discord, she thought as she saw the shutters up on his face again. What a creature of moods he was. But it was no doubt the creative spirit working in him. She could not expect him to be like other men.

He bade them goodnight outside their small cottage, and bent to kiss Aunt Millicent's cheek, then he stared at Melanie, his eyes glittering in bright moonlight.

'Sleep well. I need you feeling fresh for the work we have to do.'

'I'll be ready,' she said, steadily.

'See that you are.'

4

The following day Melanie took a rather regretful leave of the small cottage as she followed Miss Kendall out to the bus which would take them to the ship.

Once again Carlton was being helped by Bert Sloan, but Melanie was beginning to recognize the closed look on his face, which showed how much he resented having to be helped at all.

One or two of the holiday party were beginning to look at him curiously, but no one seemed to recognize him. Those who liked music seemed to prefer pop or light music. When Melanie remarked on this to Miss Kendall, the older woman nodded.

'I knew we could take a chance on it. Carl can always sort out the genuine music lovers in any case, from those who pretend, even to themselves. They turn up at concerts, earnestly following the score and showing everyone how much it means to them when all that really interests them is the image they have built up of themselves. They have horrid things to say about pop music, yet some of it is quite delightful. Don't you agree, my dear?'

Melanie nodded, inwardly amused and rather surprised. She could not imagine Miss Kendall enjoying pop music!

On board ship, Melanie almost forgot that she had work to do when she saw the beauty and luxury of her surroundings. Once again Carlton seemed almost boyish, as he turned to her.

'The Captain is giving a cocktail party in an hour,' he grinned. 'It's a conspiracy to stop me from daring to ask you to write down a single note. And in any case, it's just bribery to keep us from grumbling about lifeboat drill . . . Oh! . . .'

He made an almost strangled exclamation of surprise, and Melanie followed his gaze, her own heart leaping as the tall, magnificent figure of Marcia Dawson swayed towards them.

'Hello, darling,' she greeted Carlton, coming to put her hand through his arm and to kiss him warmly.

Melanie stepped back, but she found her own arm being gripped by Carlton so tightly that it hurt. She stood very still.

'What are you doing here, Marcia?'

The older girl turned to stare coldly at Melanie, her eyebrows slightly raised.

'Aren't you Miss Kendall's . . . er . . . companion?' she asked.

'Miss Jordan is a family friend. Her parents were close friends of my aunt's,' said Carlton. 'I'd better introduce you two properly. Miss Melanie Jordan . . . Miss Marcia Dawson.'

'How do you do?' said Melanie.

Marcia gave her a cool nod, then her interest quickened.

'Oh yes, of course I remember . . . you're the girl with . . . '

'Who is going to help me with writing down my compositions,' said

Carlton swiftly, his fingers still digging into her arm. 'You know I've decided to try my hand at composing. I did mention it.'

Marcia Dawson gave him an amused look.

'Of course, Carl. How nice for you. As you see, I decided to come on this trip after all, and there has been a cancellation on the cruise, so I flew out to join the ship. Not bad, is it? In fact . . .' her eyes flickered over Melanie again, ' . . . it might even be fun. I'll enjoy seeing how you . . . ah . . . make out.'

'Make out?'

'With your music, darling. I hope it's something I can sing. A song cycle, perhaps? No? Are you still sulking, my love? It isn't like you.'

Isn't it? wondered Melanie.

'I don't think this is a place for earnest discussion,' said Carlton, easily. 'Melanie and I are combining business with pleasure, aren't we, my dear? She inspires me.'

'I expect she does,' said Marcia, silkily.

Melanie managed to free her arm and she turned to Carlton, her eyes stormy. She disliked being used as a foil between two people who had obviously had a blazing row. They seemed to knock sparks off one another.

'Miss Kendall may want me for something,' she said, excusing herself.

Carlton put out a hand to detain her again, but she hurried away to join Miss Kendall, who was busily admiring her cabin.

'Absolutely splendid,' she said. 'The ship is fairly new, of course, and everything is quite delightful. We'll have to dress for dinner tonight, and I understand we will soon reach Mikonos. That's our first island, Melanie, and Carlton mustn't miss that. Where is he, by the way?'

'With Miss Dawson.'

'Who?'

Miss Kendall turned to stare disbelievingly at Melanie.

'Marcia Dawson. She has just joined the party because of that cancellation. I understand that she flew to Athens, in order to join the ship.'

'But she was so much against this sort of thing, and besides she . . . she shouldn't be around Carl at this time. Really, I'm very cross, very cross indeed.'

'What time?' asked Melanie.

Miss Kendall looked flustered.

'No special time. Just that Carlton is trying to get used to his injured arm and the fact that it's going to take a long time to heal is . . . is a prime factor. It might not ever be the same again.'

'Oh no!'

Melanie bit her lip, feeling a stab of pain at the thought.

'What caused the injury, Miss Kendall?' she asked, quietly.

Again the older woman looked uncomfortable.

'Carl won't talk about it, but I understand he and Marcia had a quarrel when they were having dinner together at her place. They are both such strong-minded people and they are forever quarrelling. She had wine on the table, and candles. She overdoes everything, the stupid girl, so I expect she had candles everywhere. And she had some sort of contraption for making coffee. Well, I don't know exactly what happened, and neither of them will tell me, but Carlton's sleeve caught alight and he was burned. And there might even have been a serious fire, but for him. I've no doubt she just stood there and shrieked, the silly girl, instead of helping him. Oh, he doesn't blame her, of course, but *I* blame her. I know what she is. I thought this holiday would not be her style at all, and I would get Carlton away from her for a while, but now she turns up to make mischief just when I had other plans going so well.'

'What other plans?'

'Oh . . . ' Miss Kendall flushed, and turned away. 'To get him composing, of course, with you to help him get it down in manuscript form.'

But Melanie wondered if that was all there was to Miss Kendall's plans. She looked like a naughty child caught out stealing biscuits. She kept eyeing Melanie with uncertainty.

'You're a pretty child,' she said at length, 'in fact, the more I see of you, the more I realise how pretty you are. Shelley is a knock-out, as you say, but you have true beauty which seems to grow on one. I feel sure that Carlton is beginning to realise that, too. Can't you get him away from that girl?'

'Miss Kendall!' Melanie could hardly believe her ears.

'Well . . . you needn't go to any great lengths if you'd rather not, but don't let Marcia Dawson have things all her own way. You know what I mean. I don't have to spell it out.'

Miss Kendall had plumped herself down on a chair and was looking at her beseechingly.

'I've come here to do a job,' Melanie

said, quietly, 'and that's all I want to do. I . . . I've no intention of trying to attract Mr. Kendall, even if I could. But he'd never look at me with Miss Dawson around.'

'He's a fat lot more attractive than George,' said Miss Kendall, coaxingly. 'George will be a pudding one day, and perhaps even a bath-bun as well. Carlton has a fine head of hair and takes after his father who kept all his hair until the day he died. Good hair runs in our family.'

Melanie made no reply, but deep in her heart she knew that Carlton was, indeed, a great deal more attractive than George, even if he had not a hair on his head. In fact, he was very attractive indeed!

Melanie would have enjoyed the cocktail party, the lunch, and even the lifeboat drill, if it had not been for Marcia Dawson. In a short time she had sent Carlton Kendall firmly back into his shell, so that once again he seemed more like the cool remote orchestral conductor Melanie had once known.

Miss Kendall had also lost some of her bounce but she insisted that they all join the group going by tender to Mikonos.

'It will be dark,' said Marcia, languidly. 'Carl and I know Mikonos very well, don't we, darling? We'll stay behind and I'll dress for dinner this evening. At least one can eat a good dinner aboard ship.'

'A splendid idea,' Miss Kendall enthused, 'but Carl ought to renew acquaintance with Mikonos. It's important for him to see the Islands again, isn't it, dear? It all helps while he is composing. That's so, isn't it, Carl?'

Carlton Kendall looked as though he would never be able to write another note of music. He stared at Melanie.

'Oh, for Heaven's sake . . . ' he began.

'I'll come, too,' said Marcia, sweetly. 'It could be fun, after all. I can do some shopping. I packed rather hurriedly.'

Miss Kendall said nothing, then she took Melanie's arm.

'Come on, dear, let's hope Marcia is a good sailor. The sea is quite rough.'

'If I can get a word in edgeways,' said Carlton, 'I would just like to say that I *don't* intend to go to Mikonos. It's growing dark and the sea is rough and I know the island well enough already. I have work to do . . .'

'Then I'd better stay,' said Melanie, disappointed. Although she was supposed to be working, she felt she wanted to see everything. On the other hand, she had not as yet earned a penny of her salary!

'No, you go,' he told her, 'you and Aunt Millicent, and perhaps I might have time to think!'

'Very well,' said Miss Kendall. 'Come on, dear, and we'll find something suitable to wear. We have to climb down ladders, you know, with sailors helping us into the tender. This dress is not at all suitable!'

In spite of leaving Carlton in a black

mood, Melanie could not help enjoying her trip to Mikonos. Marcia had once again changed her mind, very sweetly, indicating that Carl had probably opted to stay on board so that they could enjoy an hour or two of privacy. Bert Sloan had been sent along to help Miss Kendall with her shopping.

Melanie had expected the shops to be closed but Bert Sloan grinned when he saw the shops all opened up for business.

'They aren't going to pass up trade when a ship is in,' he said. 'Is there anything special you want, Miss Kendall?'

'Nothing you can help me to buy,' she said, her usual good humour having deserted her a little. Melanie, too, felt that some of the fun had gone out of the holiday, with Marcia Dawson's arrival.

Miss Kendall wanted an extra sweater, feeling that she had not allowed for the cool evening breezes. Melanie was more concerned to go window shopping, but Miss Kendall insisted on buying a pretty scarf. The streets were very narrow, with poor lighting, however, and Melanie felt that they had explored quite enough as they returned to the ship. Miss Kendall's energy seemed to be inexhaustible.

Melanie hesitated between two of her nicest gowns when she was dressing for dinner. The white one was her favourite, simple but elegant, but it would look better after she had acquired a tan. She'd had little opportunity for sunbathing during the early summer months in Barholme.

The other gown was very pale green, and although she had worn it a few times, it still looked fresh and pretty. Her curls were a trifle tangled after the trip to Mikonos, but Melanie brushed her hair vigorously, and applied make-up sparingly. Already she had warmth and colour in her cheeks, and the brightness of excitement in her green eyes.

'You look very nice, dear,' said Miss Kendall, approvingly, when she came to find Melanie.

'Thank you,' said Melanie, glowing with confidence.

It was short-lived, however. As they walked into the beautiful dining room, Carlton and Bert Sloan rose to greet them, and Marcia was already there. She must have spent most of her time on board preparing for this evening, thought Melanie, as she looked at the breathtakingly beautiful girl. Her black hair was piled high on her head and her magnolia skin seemed to glow in the soft lights, reflecting the lovely low-cut silk dress which was just the right shade of red.

'All dolled up, I see, Marcia,' said Miss Kendall, drily.

'Why not?' she enquired, sweetly, her black eyes roaming lazily over the older woman and Melanie. Miss Kendall had managed to look smart and neat in navy blue, but Melanie began to feel like a girl at her first school dance. She sat down rather uncomfortably as Carlton held out a chair, and again she could see the shuttered look on his face. She had been rather looking forward to beginning work with him, but now she could hardly imagine them working together. There would be no meeting of minds with Carlton Kendall in this mood.

A young Greek waiter hurried towards their table, and Melanie found her eyes following his lithe figure. He resembled some of the wonderful sculptures from Ancient Greece, she thought with interest. He caught her eye, and smiled charmingly, so that Melanie blushed furiously and looked away. To her chagrin Marcia Dawson had noticed.

'So our little secretary is susceptible,' she said, laughing. 'The handsome Angelo has made a conquest!'

Melanie found Carlton eyeing her sardonically, and again a wave of hot colour stained her cheeks.

'It's just that he . . . he looks so

. . . well . . . Greek,' she said, stammering a little.

'I know what you mean, dear,' said Miss Kendall, coming to her rescue. 'The young man looks like a Greek god. Very charming.'

'We don't stand a chance, do we, Mr. Kendall?' asked Bert Sloan, sorrowfully, and the mood at the table became considerably lightened. Carlton began to laugh.

'Not a chance, Bert.'

'There's dancing later,' said Marcia. 'That will be fun, won't it, darling?'

'Great fun,' said Carlton, without enthusiasm, though his eyes were on Melanie again.

Marcia appeared to have the healthiest of appetites, though Melanie, too, found the food delicious. Nevertheless she was more selective in what she ate, and again she noticed that Bert Sloan had managed to help Carlton without too much fuss.

Miss Kendall looked tired and Melanie wondered if the trip to

Mikonos might not have been rather too much for her.

'You young people can dance until midnight, if you wish,' she said, 'but I think I shall retire. We reach Santorini in the morning, and that's one of my favourite islands. I hope you aren't going to stay aboard, sulking, in the morning, Carl. I'm sure there must be something for you in Santorini.'

Carl glowered, then suddenly he was laughing.

'Santorini,' he said, 'the Lost City of Atlantis as a rather earnest-looking female once told me, on my first visit there. No, I mustn't miss it, and I shall want you with me along with your notebook, Melanie.'

'Oh darling, surely you can't work while we all trail around Santorini. That's ridiculous!' cried Marcia.

'I'm the best judge of that,' said Carlton, firmly. 'I said for Melanie to bring her notebook . . . where are you going?' he called to her as she rose to follow Miss Kendall.

'With Miss Kendall.'

'Don't go off with Aunt Millicent until we've had one dance at least. You must have some fun.'

Melanie bit her lip, feeling that Carlton was making a great effort to be kind, and to do his duty by her.

'The child is tired,' said Marcia. 'Let her go, Carl.'

Melanie hurried after Miss Kendall. She loved to dance, but not with Marcia looking on, and not with Carlton Kendall feeling sorry for her. Besides he was in an unpredictable mood. Anything which drew attention to his injured arm always made him withdraw into himself. He could soon lose his good humour when he tried to dance. It was better that he remain with Marcia who must, after all, know all about his injuries so that there would be no pretence between them.

'We'll be up at the crack of dawn,' Miss Kendall warned her, 'so sleep well.'

Melanie did not feel like sleeping, but

the ship made an excellent cradle, and she must have fallen asleep as soon as her head touched the pillow. Her last thoughts were with Carlton, and Marcia Dawson, and then George who was so far away. How was Mrs. Price and Shelley faring at Jordan's? Was everything as it should be, or were the problems already piling up? Melanie sighed and punched her pillow. Even on such a wonderful cruise, she could not escape the realities of life.

★　★　★

Melanie found herself being pulled out of bed at dawn the following morning by Miss Kendall, who was full of excitement and anticipation.

'Come on, up you get dear. The tender is due to leave at seven-thirty and we must have breakfast . . .'

'Oh . . . breakfast . . .' said Melanie, who had never felt less like it.

'You'd better have something to sustain you,' said Miss Kendall, briskly.

'Sustain me?' repeated Melanie, still doped with sleep.

'Yes. Santorini is by way of being your first Greek Island since it was too dark to see much of Mikonos. Oh, I admit that we purchased goods in the shops and walked the narrow streets, but we could see little else. Now you are going to see some really worthwhile scenery.'

Melanie was becoming more and more wide awake as excitement gripped her. She suddenly experienced a great rush of affection for the older lady.

'Oh, Miss Kendall, how good you are to me!'

'Nonsense, my dear. You'll earn it, if only you can help Carl. Don't forget he wants you to take notes today.'

'But sometimes I feel that you, or perhaps Miss Dawson, could do it so much better.'

'I'm not accurate enough, and can you really see Marcia stirring herself in order to further someone else's career other than her own?'

Melanie said nothing. She did not know the other girl well enough to make a judgement, and she suspected Miss Kendall might be prejudiced, but surely . . . if Marcia Dawson had been even in a small degree responsible for Carlton's accident, wouldn't she *want* to help him? Melanie felt that there was a great deal more to that accident than Miss Kendall knew.

From the first she had suspected that they were in love, even if Carlton tried to fight this at times. Perhaps that was the main reason why he hated his disability so much. It debarred him from conducting so that his career lay in ruins, but it could be redeemed if he started composing successfully. Perhaps he preferred not to accept help from Marcia because of pride. He may want to have a successful new career before thinking of marriage.

Marcia did not make an appearance for breakfast and Melanie was pleased to see Carlton in a happy mood. He looked younger and more vulnerable, clad in maroon slacks and a white polo-necked sweater.

'I've put everything I need in this briefcase,' Melanie told him.

'Oh, leave it,' he said. 'I was only teasing you. Perhaps we can do something when we get back from Santorini, but I just want to refresh my memory of the place. I want to get all my own ideas and impressions gathered together before we get anything down on paper. It's your first visit to Santorini, so let's just enjoy it.'

'Isn't Miss Dawson coming?' she asked.

His smile faded a little.

'Marcia knows Greece well enough already. She . . . we were rather late last night.'

Melanie was surprised to find herself experiencing a stab of jealousy. She had a sudden vision of Marcia, as she had looked the previous evening, dancing in Carlton's arms. No doubt his injury had not been such a handicap!

'What's wrong now?' he was asking. 'You're such a moody girl.'

Moody! He was a fine one to talk! she thought.

'Nothing, I'm fine,' she assured him.

'Good. We'd best get going then, into the tender before . . .'

'Before?'

'Before we get left behind,' he grinned, though she suspected that he had been about to say something else.

Santorini was not real, thought Melanie, as the tender neared the island and she looked up at tiny whitewashed houses on the top of high cliffs.

'Oh, isn't it enchanting!' she said.

'I thought you'd like it,' Carlton told her, boyishly as they stepped ashore at a small port. There were a few small shops, but Melanie's eyes were drawn to the stone steps which wound up to the top of the cliffs. At the foot of the steps a collection of mules stood waiting silently, while a yelling Greek kept them in order with a switch.

'Look,' she said, pointing. 'Why do you think he needs those mules?'

'You'll see in a moment,' Carlton

grinned. 'We ride to the top of the cliffs on those mules. Yours is going to be fortunate, but one or two of the little creatures less so.'

He raised an eyebrow as he looked round at one of two well-built members of the party.

'Oh, surely we don't have to ride on a mule!' she protested.

'Why not? They've been trained to carry us up the cliffs, and the alternative for you would be to hang about waiting for us all to come back. You would miss seeing most of the island, you know.'

'Well . . .' she began, wondering how much to believe as she caught a gleam in his eyes. 'Well, I'll go, of course, if that's the only means of transport. But I shan't like it!'

The mules with their burdens rode three abreast up the cliffs, and after a horrified look at the sheer drop down the rocks to the sea, Melanie closed her eyes and wished that Miss Kendall had not persuaded her to eat breakfast!

She patted her small animal to encourage him, wishing she could speak Greek in order to tell the owner of the mules exactly what she thought of him, especially when he yelled at the animals and flicked at them with his switch.

'Cheer up, it isn't as bad as it sounds,' Carlton said beside her. 'He probably loves them all devotedly.'

'I don't believe it,' she said, gritting her teeth.

'Well, never mind, we've made it,' said Carlton, as they reached the top of the cliffs.

Although it was still early, the merchants had all their goods displayed, ready for business, though Melanie was more interested in the quaint houses.

'Do they live in the back of the houses, and use the front as stalls of a sort?' she asked Carlton.

'Certainly. Have you brought your camera?'

'No, I did not think about it. I . . . I

rather assumed I should be doing more work.'

'Don't worry, you'll have plenty of work to do when the mood takes me,' he said, easily.

'You're a creature of moods,' she said, unthinkingly, then felt embarrassed. She was so inclined to put her foot in it!

'Pot calling kettle black,' he told her. 'You're a moody little person yourself . . . all meek and mild one moment, then raging at people the next.'

'Sorry.'

'So you should be. Look, don't you find this beaten chain belt attractive?'

'Beautiful,' Melanie agreed, then her eyes were caught by a selection of Greek Island dolls.

'Oh, how pretty,' she said.

'Choose one,' Carlton told her, 'on me.'

'I . . . I'd rather buy it for myself,' she said, pride welling up in her. She did not want to accept any more from the Kendalls until she had earned her keep.

'Suit yourself,' he told her, coolly, but she felt he was rather hurt.

'Well . . . all right. It was nice of you to offer. I'm sorry.'

He shrugged, but did not renew his offer, and Melanie bought the brightly-coloured doll herself.

Miss Kendall and Bert Sloan had wandered on ahead. It was almost as though the older woman was determined to throw her and Carlton together, Melanie thought with embarrassment. She did not want to be used by Miss Kendall to annoy Marcia Dawson!

'Would you like to see through this Church?' Carlton asked, as they walked along together. He had already taken several pictures of the island, and promised to give some of them to Melanie as a souvenir.

'Yes,' she agreed.

The Church was beautiful and full of peace. Carlton reached out and took her hand as they wandered round silently. She felt that he was listening again for the music from deep within himself, and she did not want to interrupt the spell. His hand was cool and firm as he gripped hers, and suddenly she wanted this moment to last and last.

Silently she prayed for his well-being and happiness, and for the healing of his arm which must, surely, also heal his spirit. She glanced up at him and found that her heart was beating madly so that she could scarcely breathe. He looked cool and remote once more, but she knew she loved him as she would love no other man.

'What are you thinking, Melanie?' he asked her.

Her fingers trembled in his.

'I . . . I was thinking you probably hear your music again,' she said, huskily.

'Was that all?'

'Y . . . yes.'

'I don't believe you.'

He turned to face her, then suddenly there was a great deal of chatter and laughter as a crowd of sight-seers entered the church.

'Damn!' said Carlton.

'That's swearing . . . in Church, too.'

'Come on,' he told her. 'Sometimes I love the anonymity of this holiday, then I feel crowded again. Now I feel very crowded indeed.'

Outside he fished into his pocket and brought out the metal belt.

'For you,' he said, smiling.

'Oh . . . how lovely . . . but . . .'

'In the Middle Ages men presented their ladies with chastity belts,' he said, his eyes twinkling.

'Hardly relevant,' she said in return, but she thanked him prettily and very sincerely for the gift.

'And here's another,' he said, producing a tiny silver charm of a mule.

'Just to remind you of the climb up the cliffs.'

'Oh . . . how very pretty . . . but I doubt if I'll ever need to be reminded about that climb!'

'It was a bit hair-raising for you.'

'Do we walk back down?' she asked.

'No. You can walk, of course, but you may have to pick your way rather delicately through the mire. I think we'd better ride down. You'll just have to be brave again.'

Melanie made no reply, though suddenly she was wildly happy, happier and more alive than she had been since before her father died. What a wonderful companion Carlton Kendall could be when he wished. If only . . . if only it was always like this.

'It's been a wonderful morning,' she said. 'I love it here. It's like an island of enchantment.'

'Perhaps we'll come back one day,' said Carlton, softly.

Melanie did not reply. When she returned to Barholme, no doubt her feet would be firmly planted back on the ground again. There would be little room for enchantment then.

'There you go . . . back into those thoughts of yours again,' said Carlton. 'What are you thinking about?'

'Barholme. Everything that is still waiting for me there.'

His mood began to change.

'Yes. The Scots have a saying for it . . . 'Old clothes and porridge' . . . or something similar.'

She could have quoted the saying in the vernacular, but she merely nodded. Santorini had been beautiful, but it was not part of her world.

On board ship they found Marcia looking angry and frustrated. She hurried forward accusingly to Carlton.

'So you went after all! Last night you had decided you would give it all a miss and leave it to the tourists. That's what you said, isn't it?'

'That was before I remembered that *I'm* a tourist,' said Carlton, grinning. 'I wanted to refresh my memories of Santorini, Marcia.'

'You could have woken me up, darling.'

'And lose you your beauty sleep! I'm sure the rest would do you the world of good. You have worked even harder than I have before this break, and you deserve a good rest.'

'What are you doing now?' Marcia asked.

'I deserve a rest, too, and so does Melanie. She felt as though she were standing on her head getting up and down the cliffs. She says that coming down was even worse than going up. Now, we'll find ourselves some nice deck chairs, then after a rest and a cool drink, we'll get down to doing some work.'

Marcia turned to stare again at Melanie.

'Quite a job you've found for yourself, Miss Jordan,' she said. 'Doesn't it ever puzzle you as to why you should be so fortunate? I shouldn't have thought that a young girl like you would have gained quite so much experience.'

It had occurred to Melanie time after time that she was, indeed, fortunate.

'I . . . er . . .' she began, but a glance at Carlton stilled her tongue.

'Aunt Millicent and I still like to make our own arrangements, Marcia,' he said, coldly and again her eyes slanted at him knowingly.

'Are you lunching in the dining room, or have smorgasbord in the lounge?' she asked.

'Smorgasbord, I expect. Come on, Melanie, I want to start now. You'll have to wait for your rest. The mood is on me.'

Melanie began to earn her salary, glad she had had such a sound training in music. That, surely, would be the best qualification of all for being given the job and she would make sure that Marcia knew it one of these days.

Carlton had been given permission to make use of the piano in the lounge, and as the notes seemed to pour from him, Melanie wrote them down and played small passages over to him again and again, altering and repeating according to his dictation. She forgot her surroundings, her hunger and her fatigue as she worked steadily with Carlton until he finally called a halt.

At one time she remembered Miss Kendall coming to find her, and Marcia's imperious voice raised petulantly in complaint. But she did not care. The music was wonderful. Carlton might be moody and bad-tempered and he might treat her with scant consideration, but she was happy to forgive him anything.

This wonderful music was being created from the depth of his being, and Melanie felt humble that she was contributing even a small part of it. As well as loving him for himself, she was in awe of his creative powers.

'It's . . . it's wonderful,' she said, softly after he paused, tired and spent.

'You're a competent pianist, but that's all,' he told her rather irritably after he asked her to play it over yet again. 'It will sound better when someone who is really inspired plays it.'

She flushed, her heart plunging. He could be really hurtful at times, she thought, resentfully. They had seemed to work almost with one mind, and now all he could do was to criticize her playing.

'I'm sorry I don't come up to standard.'

'Oh, calm down. Your red hair is standing on end. You're splendidly competent at the job I've hired you to do . . . helping me to get all my ideas down on paper. Come on and don't sulk. I can't say you're a marvellous pianist when you're no such thing, can I? Come on and let's see if there's anything left on the plates for lunch. I'm starving.'

Marcia found them again while they were eating in one of the lounges.

'So you've surfaced,' she said, smiling sweetly at Carlton. 'Darling, you surely are not serious about composing, as a career I mean? You're so much more talented as a musician or a conductor.'

'You forget that I've got an injured arm,' said Carlton, harshly.

'Oh, but that's only temporary. It should be better soon now, shouldn't it? I mean, you've had it bandaged long enough really. We could do with getting back to work. We work so well together, you and I.'

She stared meaningfully at Melanie in case that she, too, felt that she worked well with Carlton.

'I don't mind you doing a song cycle though. It might take very well, but I don't know about a . . . a . . . '

'Tone poem?'

'Is that what you have in mind?'

'No, I want to do more than that.'

'Aren't you being a little bit ambitious?'

Melanie saw the familiar closed look coming over Carlton's face.

'Don't be so discouraging,' she said, sharply.

Her quick temper had let her down again, she thought rather tiredly, as Marcia turned slowly to stare at her again, as though she couldn't believe her ears.

'And aren't you being rather impertinent, Miss . . . ah . . . Jordan?' she asked. 'You should learn better manners, and especially you should learn not to interrupt when old friends are talking.'

'Sorry,' mumbled Melanie, scarlet-faced. 'Er . . . if you don't need me any more for the moment, Mr. Kendall, I shall go and find Miss Kendall.'

Carlton nodded, staring at her almost without recognition. He looked very pale and tired after the effort he had put in with his music. It did not come easy to him, and he was a perfectionist who obviously worked at every little phrase until he got it right.

'Miss Kendall is getting herself primed for a visit to Crete,' said Marcia. 'She wants value for the money she has spent on this holiday, down to the last penny. Remember that, Miss Jordan.'

Melanie turned and walked towards her cabin.

5

'It's Greek night tonight on board,' said Miss Kendall. 'We are all obliged to wear something Greek and after dinner the crew is going to entertain with Greek dances. That must surely provide more inspiration for Carl. How is the work going? Have you done some good work together, dear?'

'Oh yes, quite good,' said Melanie rather listlessly.

'What has happened now? Have you two been quarrelling?'

'No, I'm just tired, that's all,' said Melanie. 'It has all been so exciting, and I suppose one gets a certain amount of reaction.'

Miss Kendall would probably find out that she'd had words with Marcia, but she was not going to hear it from Melanie.

'Poor child. I rather dragged you out

of bed, didn't I? Never mind, you must be fresh for Crete. We put into port there, so we'll have more time on the island and there are some splendid ruins of ancient civilizations for you to see.'

Miss Kendall kept well up to date with every aspect of the cruise. Melanie might have been amused if she had not still felt irritated and upset by Marcia. What did the older girl mean by the very pointed remarks she kept making about Miss Kendall wanting full value for her money? It was almost as though Melanie would be expected to pay for this holiday in ways she would not like!

'You're being very kind to me, Miss Kendall,' she said, slowly and thoughtfully.

'You're Alex's daughter.'

'Is that the only reason?' Melanie asked, bluntly.

'Whatever do you mean, child?'

'Nothing,' Melanie muttered. 'I'm sorry.'

'No, tell me what is on your mind.'

'I wondered if there could . . . well . . . if there could be anything else you might want from me?'

Miss Kendall coloured like a beetroot.

'Why do you ask such a question? Who's been talking to you? Not Carlton, I'm quite sure.'

'Miss Dawson keeps dropping hints that . . . that you want something. I don't understand her remarks at times.'

Miss Kendall seemed to have lost her tongue.

'That girl!' she said at length. 'It's only dreams, dear . . . dreams and schemes of an old woman, but I *can* dream, can't I? If only you and Carlton would fall in love! I'm sure you'd be so right for one another.'

Melanie's heart beat so fast that it threatened to suffocate her.

'Oh, Miss Kendall . . . '

'I wish you would call me Aunt Millicent.'

She had never been the sort of woman Melanie felt she could call 'aunt'.

113

'I . . . I'll try to remember,' Melanie said, huskily, 'but I've always thought of you as Miss Kendall.'

'You're changing the subject. Don't you find Carlton attractive at all? If you must know, I schemed for this cruise, arranging for you to work for him and hoping that if you were thrown together with a common interest between you, then you might be attracted to one another. You're a very lovely girl, and he's an attractive enough man. He won't always be disabled, you know . . . I'm quite sure he won't.'

'That wouldn't matter,' said Melanie, quickly, then she could have bitten out her tongue when she saw the hope springing into Miss Kendall's eyes. Really, this was ridiculous! Carlton Kendall had no regard for her in that way, and even though they had spent a happy morning in Santorini, he had just been amusing himself and seeking young companionship. She thought that half of the trouble between him and Marcia was because he could not help being in love with the beautiful singer, but hated his injuries. If his arm had not been injured, they might even be married by now. But it had been injured, and if it did not heal perfectly, Marcia Dawson might be revolted by his scars. Perhaps the shock of his injuries made him try to fight against love and turned him to someone like Melanie whom he would never have noticed in ordinary circumstances.

'Then you are becoming good friends?' asked Miss Kendall, eagerly.

'We get along better than I would ever have thought possible, but that's all,' said Melanie firmly. 'Really, you shouldn't be trying to arrange Carlton's life for him like this . . . or mine, for that matter. Does he know you feel this way? I mean, surely he isn't a party to . . . '

'Of course he isn't! He won't even discuss his feelings with me, but I know him very well, because I love him very much. I didn't know what else to do for him after that terrible accident. He was so . . . so shattered. He is *still* shattered inside. I was willing to try anything . . . anything . . . to help him, even having crazy ideas about you, child. Forgive me. The working part of the holiday may prove the best notion I've had yet, though. He seems to be genuinely excited about that, and from what I saw, you were working well together. Didn't you feel that he has the power within him? Didn't you feel that he has that little extra something which is everything.'

Melanie nodded. 'Yes, he has the gift.'

'Then help him, dear. Help him all you can. Never mind my silly ideas. I'm just a stupid old woman at times. No wonder Alex loved me, but was never in love with me. I was older than he anyway, and I was never beautiful like Betty. Marcia Dawson is beautiful, too, but a great deal of Betty's beauty was sheer goodness of heart. She was a very gentle girl, but you have a great deal of your father in you, and you would need that to deal with Carlton. One needs to stand up to him, as well as helping him. Promise me you'll try.'

'I'll do my best,' said Melanie.

Later as she rested she felt strangely touched that Miss Kendall should want her for Carlton, who was her whole life. Melanie had nothing, except herself. The business was rocky, and she had not managed to make her name on the concert platform as she had hoped and dreamed might happen one day. She did not have that extra something. She was ordinary Melanie Jordan, and Marcia would have more to offer, as a wife, for someone like Carl. Marcia's own fame would reflect on him, and would keep his name before the public.

Yet Miss Kendall probably knew that she would love Carl more than Marcia, who in the long run, loved herself best of all.

Melanie could only remember Carl's dark eyes smiling into hers when he gave her the pretty belt and the tiny mule charm. She would treasure them all her life, she thought, as she drifted off to sleep.

★　★　★

Melanie chose to wear her simple white dress with the Greek belt. Her skin had now been touched by the sun so that it glowed like ripe peaches, and she brushed her dark chestnut hair into shining curls.

'You look beautiful,' Miss Kendall told her, with satisfaction. 'I'm proud of you.'

Marcia Dawson had chosen nasturtium pink and once again she looked breathtakingly lovely, though her eyes darted towards Melanie, sweeping over the girl from head to foot, when they all met in the dining room.

'Trying to be a Greek goddess, Miss Jordan?' she asked. 'I see you are a hunter of souvenirs.'

Melanie said nothing, feeling that Carlton would not like her to tell Marcia how she had acquired the belt.

'I find it very attractive,' she said, quietly and Carlton smiled at her warmly.

'Melanie is very unspoilt, Marcia,' he said, softly.

'I find all that sort of thing rather boring,' said Marcia. 'I suppose we *have* to listen to all the Greek entertainment this evening?'

'I can't help feeling you should not have been so eager to come on this cruise, Marcia,' said Miss Kendall. 'Nothing seems to suit you whatsoever.'

'Oh, but I find quite a lot of things amusing,' said Marcia sweetly. 'I just don't enjoy the sort of thing I'm *told* to enjoy. I do like to choose for myself.'

'Fortunately everyone doesn't feel as you do,' Miss Kendall said, equably, 'therefore we won't be deprived of something very colourful and enjoyable.'

Marcia shrugged, and turned pointedly to Carlton.

'I would like to talk to you about something, Carl darling. Do we *have* to go into the lounge after dinner to watch all this Greek entertainment?'

Carlton was looking at her as though his thoughts were miles away.

'Carl! I'm talking to you!'

'What? Oh . . . sorry, Marcia, I was just working something out in my mind. What was it, my dear?'

'Are you going into the lounge after dinner to watch the crew amusing us with Greek dances and playing Greek music?'

'Of course,' said Carlton. 'I look forward to it very much.'

Melanie saw the light of mischief in Miss Kendall's eyes, and the look of amusement which passed between the older woman and her nephew. Carlton had been listening all the time, she thought! He just chose this way of answering Marcia's query out of devilment. Did he think that the best way of holding Marcia was to keep her on tenterhooks?

'Oh, all right,' she was grumbling. 'We're moving towards Turkey now, aren't we? It's Rhodes next, isn't it?'

They had all had a wonderful time on Crete, though Melanie's feeling of enchantment seemed to vanish with Marcia's presence. She knew that she wanted Carlton to herself, but Marcia was beginning to look at her with more speculation and she knew that Santorini would soon be just like a dream.

'It's Rhodes,' Miss Kendall was saying.

'I think we should all visit the Grand Master's castle,' said Marcia, her mood changing so that her dazzling smile enveloped all of them.

'I may not go to Rhodes,' said Miss Kendall. 'I sometimes feel that the natives laugh at the tourists. I think they are developing their tourist area too fast.'

'Oh, Aunt Millicent, you're the limit,' said Carlton. 'You always want to be different.'

'Very well. We visit the Grand Master's castle, if only because I don't want Melanie to be lost in the place. We might never see her again!'

'And that would be a tragedy, wouldn't it, Miss Kendall?' asked Marcia, roguishly, though she seemed to emphasize every word.

Again Miss Kendall seemed to bristle angrily.

'It would be a tragedy if *any* of us came to any harm while we were on holiday, Marcia,' she said, quietly, 'or at any other time for that matter. But holidays are arranged to benefit people, not dispose of them.'

'You two choose strange topics of conversation at times,' said Carlton. 'Would anyone care for more wine. You, Bert?'

'That ouzo tastes like licorice to me,' said Bert Sloan.

Carlton laughed. 'You'll acquire a taste for it before the tour is finished, Bert, never fear.'

In the lounge Melanie watched the entertainment with fascination, finding herself beating time to the rhythm of the music, as the dancers swayed and stamped their feet. Her eyes were shining as she turned to find Carlton watching her instead of the music. Melanie's heart gave a great leap as their eyes met, and she saw that his dark eyes were brilliant and were holding hers as though by a magnet.

Then Marcia moved forward to sit beside Carlton and his mood changed. Just what was there between them? wondered Melanie, feeling that the time was coming when she had to know for sure. She had been content to love him from afar, but now she was gradually realising that it would not be enough. She wanted to feel his arms round her, and to belong to him, and her love was growing purely selfish. Marcia didn't deserve him. Marcia wouldn't look after him as well as she could.

But what did Carlton really feel in that complicated heart of his? Was he in love with Marcia and not averse to amusing himself with any other girl who appeared in his orbit? He must have had hundreds of girls adoring him when he was conducting the Caledonian Orchestra, and his recording of the Max Bruch's Violin Concerto had sold in its thousands . . . or so she would have thought. At least, it had sold well enough in Jordan's.

Her gaze went to his arm as she wondered if the exercises he did every day with Bert Sloan were having any effect. He *must* get better soon . . . he must!, she found herself thinking, then her eyes were drawn to his again. This time he gave her his withdrawn brooding gaze.

'I would like to go to my cabin,' said Miss Kendall in her ear. 'You young people stay by all means.'

'No, I prefer to come with you,' said Melanie, quickly.

'But Melanie! Oh, very well, dear, come with me by all means. We have many places still to visit. There is plenty of time for you to . . . well . . . to have a good time,' she ended, lamely.

She meant that there would be plenty of time to throw her at Carlton's head!

thought Melanie grimly. Miss Kendall must be raving mad to start scheming like this. She was no more suited to Carlton Kendall than a sparrow to a peacock!

Yet, if only they had met under different circumstances, they might have become such good friends, she thought wistfully. He could make her feel so alive.

At least Marcia was pleased to see them go, but Bert Sloan was also removing himself discreetly. Marcia could have Carlton all to herself.

6

Marcia still seemed to have kept her good humour as they all walked ashore at Rhodes the following morning. The island was crowded with holiday-makers sun-bathing on the sands and Miss Kendall looked at the crowded beaches a trifle doubtfully.

'I don't like crowds,' she said. 'I should have stayed on board ship.'

'I thought you wanted to see a castle,' said Melanie.

'The Grand Master's Castle . . . once the home of the Knights of St. John,' said Miss Kendall, as she plunged along in the wake of Marcia, with Carlton bringing up the rear, having paused for a word with Bert Sloan. 'It was destroyed then rebuilt by the Italians during the war. Ouch! Now young man, watch out where you are throwing your ball.'

Miss Kendall caught a beach ball against her ample chest, then handed it back to the elder of two small boys who were also enjoying the tour along with their parents. The children's parents hurried forward to apologize, and Melanie waited, looking round at the brightness of the sun sparkling on the sea and the white buildings which lay beyond.

She caught sight of Marcia Dawson speaking quickly to one or two people, then there seemed to be a movement of the crowds ahead, and an earnest-looking girl with straight dark hair dressed in a chignon caught hold of her arm.

'Is that Carlton Kendall?' she asked, panting. 'Is it really Kendall, the conductor?'

'Why ... ye ... yes,' said Melanie, taken aback, and a moment later she was thrust aside while a party of autograph hunters began to surround Carl. Somehow Marcia Dawson was included as they swarmed around, offering anything handy on which he could write his autograph. Melanie caught Carlton's eyes on her, glaring at her balefully.

'You should not have told those girls who Carlton was, dear,' said Miss Kendall, chidingly. 'If one doesn't draw people's attention to Carl, then he usually manages to go around unrecognized. He hates this sort of fuss.'

'Oh, but I didn't . . .' began Melanie. 'At least . . . I was asked . . .'

'He appreciates that it's part of the price he has to pay, of course, but he doesn't go out of his way to invite this sort of thing. Please do remember that.'

She saw Bert Sloan trying to hold back one or two people who were crowding against Carlton's arm. She suspected they were not all lovers of orchestral music, but the chance to get the autograph of a celebrity seemed to have swept through the crowds, and Carlton was being besieged on all sides, also Marcia Dawson who had become separated from them.

Bert Sloan began to take charge, explaining that Mr. Kendall could write no more owing to his arm injury, and soon he was guiding Carlton to a small café where he managed to dodge the remainder of the crowds.

Miss Kendall dragged Melanie along behind her, and they managed to reach Carlton's side. She saw from his white face that his arm was hurting because of the crowds, and his efforts to make some sort of signature.

'You little fool!' he said to Melanie. 'Whatever possessed you to go blabbing like that? I saw you telling that girl with the black hair. No one bothers about me normally. It only takes one, and they all think they are missing something.'

'But . . . the girl asked . . . ' said Melanie, lamely, then her chin lifted. 'I think Miss Dawson told them.'

'Then you're out of your mind,' said Marcia, behind her.

The singer's hair was disarrayed and she had torn the sleeve of her dress. 'If you think I enjoy being messed up and having my clothing ripped, you must be mad.'

Melanie said nothing. She felt her throat going thick with tears as she realized they were all blaming her. Yet deep down she was sure that it was Marcia who had set it all up. She knew that Rhodes was very popular as a tourist area, and there would be quite a few English people on the beach who would recognize Carl and herself . . . but only after they were prompted! And Melanie was convinced that Marcia had done the prompting.

'We'll take it easy, darling,' she was saying to Carl, 'and not risk injury to your arm again. I know my way around. We'll find a quiet spot until it's time to go back to the ship.'

Miss Kendall nodded after a moment's thought.

'Perhaps that would be best. Melanie, you can come with me. We might as well do the tour now that we are here, but I think Marcia is right and that Carl needs to get his breath back.'

Melanie was glad when they reached the old city within the walls of the fortress, and after a while she forgot about the bad start to her visit and was fascinated by all the jewellery shops and windows full of gold and silver.

'Perhaps we'll come back one day,' Miss Kendall said. 'Each island can only be explored properly by spending one's whole holiday in one of the villages.'

Melanie nodded a trifle regretfully. She was never likely to come back to Rhodes. She had wanted to go to the Mandraki Harbour with Carlton, where once again they could have absorbed the atmosphere, but now she felt that the friendship and liking which had been building up between them had gone. She was just a nuisance to him again, a girl foisted on to him by his aunt in a pathetic attempt to help him.

Yet she could not help feeling that Marcia had done all this, she thought, as she lay down to sleep that night, and again her temper began to boil. She was not going to be made to look a fool, she decided rebelliously. She would play Marcia Dawson at her own game.

News that Carlton Kendall and Marcia Dawson were well-known on the concert platform seemed to spread round the ship, and the following evening Marcia was prevailed upon to supply the entertainment. Carlton had politely declined and there were murmurs of sympathy when people realised that his injured arm was a greater handicap to him than to most people.

'I can't sing,' said Marcia. 'I have no accompanist.'

'Melanie will play for you,' said Miss Kendall, sweetly. 'You can play, can't you, child?'

'I . . . I hardly think I'm up to standard,' said Melanie, looking cautiously at Carlton, who did not bother to disagree with her.

'We aren't critical,' said one of the passengers who had already entertained the party with conjuring tricks.

'Oh, very well,' said Marcia, and managed to find some music. She chose simple ballads which were very popular, so that Melanie thought that it was very fortunate that she had the music handy. She was quite well used to playing accompaniments, and was determined not to give Marcia any cause for complaint. At the same time, she was lost in admiration for the rich quality of the other girl's voice.

'That was beautiful,' she said, sincerely, and for once Marcia gave her a genuine smile.

'You play quite well,' she conceded. 'Shall we try 'A Brown Bird Singing'?'

'One of my favourites,' said Melanie.

How could Carlton fail to be charmed by such a voice? Melanie wondered, after the applause had died away and Marcia went to sit beside Carlton.

'Bodrum in the morning,' Miss Kendall was saying. 'We must be up early again, Melanie.'

She nodded quietly. Carlton Kendall

seemed to have shelved his plans for composing music, and she was more a companion to Miss Kendall than anything else. What would happen after they returned to London? Would he still expect her to take dictation before going back home to Barholme, or had he lost interest?

Fervently she hoped he had not given up the idea. In her depressed moments she was inclined to think that it was one of Miss Kendall's schemes, but even now the melody from the first piece he had dictated was in her mind, sometimes elusive, but always enchanting! He was a wonderful composer and must have so much to give the world. Surely he must carry on with such work.

Miss Kendall wanted all of them to visit Bodrum, and once again Melanie found herself enjoying the day too much to worry about what lay beyond.

Carlton bought both girls a pair of harem shoes and camel shoes for Miss Kendall. Melanie turned the tables by buying him a pipe, and saw the faint look of hostility back in Marcia's eyes. Since the concert, she had been almost friendly, having appreciated the younger girl's genuine admiration.

'Aren't you writing any postcards, Melanie?' she asked, pointing to a table on the waterfront, and a little box where stamps were dispensed. There were a couple of rickety chairs where Melanie could sit down to write her cards.

'Oh . . . well . . . I suppose I could,' she said. 'I'll send one to Mrs. Price and Shelley.'

'Who?' asked Marcia. 'Did you say Shelley Price?'

'Yes. Do you know her?'

Marcia's eyes had grown even more calculating.

'She is . . . or was . . . another of Carl's lame ducks not so long ago. Only I had the impression that *that* young lady could very well take care of herself.'

'Carl's . . . lame ducks?' asked Melanie.

'Sure. He keeps finding them. You know the sort of thing I mean; poor little girls down on their luck. Not that it applies to *you*, my dear, I'm quite sure,' added Marcia, sweetly, 'and don't tell Carl I called his dear little Shelley a lame duck, or Miss Kendall either for that matter. They don't like me to refer to people as their 'lame ducks' yet the expression describes them all admirably.'

'Oh, of . . . of course,' said Melanie.

So she wasn't the only one the Kendalls had helped. She was just another girl among many. For another reason, too, she felt strangely uneasy. She had not realised that Shelley Price was friendly with Carlton, yet she ought to have realized this. After all, Miss Kendall and Mrs. Price were old friends. And the girl was so beautiful . . . even lovelier than Marcia. There had been times when Melanie had felt that Carlton and Marcia were not really suited to one another and there might be hope for her after all, but now she was beginning to feel a new jealousy.

'Were they special friends . . . Carlton and Shelley Price?' she asked.

'Oh, there will always be that sort of girl in Carl's life,' said Marcia, carelessly. 'He's an artist, after all.'

They were shepherded into a small minibus driven by a crazy driver who seemed to take a delight in scattering people and animals, not to mention driving within an inch of front doors, but Melanie took it all calmly. She had too much to think about.

The man who could do conjuring tricks spent a few happy moments taking eggs out of the ears of the children in one of the villages. Melanie smiled at one small boy, who ran and hid behind his mother's skirts as she went to milk their goat. They lived simple lives, thought Melanie, half-enviously. Her own problems were probably only small to them. She had fallen in love with the wrong man, and her normal everyday life was going to seem even more dull because of it.

On impulse she had sent a card to George, and had found Carlton looking over her shoulder as she posted it.

'Hope to see you soon,' he quoted. 'Are you so fed up already?'

'*I'm* not fed up,' she said, 'but I think you are. And, anyway, you shouldn't be reading my postcards.'

'Don't presume to know how I feel,' he told her, and she flushed. He was an expert at putting her in her place.

The ship was due to return to Athens the following day, and that evening everyone was in a merry mood as they all attended the Captain's dinner.

'I'll never eat all this,' said Melanie as plate after plate of exotic food was placed before her. She had enjoyed the Greek food, but found it rather rich in olive oil as Miss Kendall had predicted.

'Of course you will,' said Carlton.

Normally she found herself sitting between Miss Kendall and Bert Sloan, but this evening, without quite knowing how it had happened, she found Carlton sitting beside her, his eyes alight with fun. He looked happy again, and was becoming more adept at using his left hand so that he was enjoying everything hugely.

There was to be a concert later in the lounge, with games to follow, and once again Marcia had been asked to sing, but this time she declined. There was a limit to her generosity.

'I start a tour of the United States as soon as I get back,' she said. 'I don't see why you can't come along, Carl, under the circumstances we discussed earlier. I don't see why you had to cancel everything. After all, your arm is responding very well to treatment now, and I know you're beginning to use it a little.'

Some of the fun went out of his eyes.

'I have my own plans made, Marcia,' he told her. 'They don't include a tour which would be just a hazard. I don't need another break. This has been the best holiday I've had for ages, and I intend to go on to Athens and Istanbul before flying home. I know I've been a

139

bad-tempered bear at times, but I do feel the better for it.'

'But do you *have* to go trailing round sight-seeing after the cruise?' asked Marcia. 'Haven't you had enough of that? You know I've got to fly back to London to prepare for my tour. Why can't you come with me, and we could have a happy time in London? After all, darling, if we're going to be apart for ages . . . '

Melanie's cheeks were pink. Marcia's rich voice was very penetrating, and she felt like an eavesdropper without having any choice in the matter. She could feel Carlton moving restlessly beside her.

'I'm not ready to go home yet, Marcia,' he said, quietly. 'In spite of appearances to the contrary, I really am working . . . '

'It's that girl, isn't it?' she muttered in a low voice, though it was still audible to Melanie, who moved restlessly along with Carl to show that she could hear.

'I can't discuss it with you,' Carlton

140

said, but Melanie suspected that this was because he was now aware that she could hear every word they said.

'You know how I felt . . . feel . . . about your injury, darling,' Marcia said, a catch in her voice. 'You know I don't think I'll ever be able to get over it. It was just too awful.'

'We won't discuss that either,' said Carlton, harshly, and Melanie could hear the other girl catch her breath.

'So you *still* blame me!'

'Placing blame is a useless occupation. I prefer to build on adversity, and not rake over the ashes.'

'It doesn't pay to marry for . . . for security only.'

'I hope you will never do such a thing then,' said Carlton.

'Oh, you know what I mean!' said Marcia, crossly.

'I told you, I don't want to discuss it. Enjoy your dinner, my dear. I've lost count, but we must be nearly up to twenty courses.'

He turned to Melanie.

141

'What? Don't tell me you've lost your appetite?'

'Something like that,' she said, coolly.

At least Carlton had not encouraged Marcia Dawson to talk about her behind her back, but there was a great deal in the conversation which she would have preferred not to overhear. But who was marrying whom for security only? She pondered the remark, but could make no sense of it.

The passenger who was a magician became the star turn of the concert later and produced Miss Kendall's handkerchief and ball point pen from behind Marcia's ear. A young girl sang folk songs and strummed a guitar, but no one thought of asking Melanie to play, rather to her relief. She was never at her best with concerts of this kind.

Later that night Miss Kendall realized that she had left her spectacles in the lounge, and asked Melanie to go and pick them up. It was very late and only a very few people were still around, one woman offering to help

Melanie in her search for the spectacles.

'Here they are, my dear,' she said, finding that they had slipped down the side of one of the seats.

'Oh, thank you,' Melanie said, relieved. Miss Kendall liked to have all her belongings around her.

'Don't go back just yet!' said Carlton behind her. 'I never get a chance to talk to you. Come up on deck and look at the Moon. No one will trouble us.'

'Oh, but Miss Kendall will want her reading glasses.'

'Nonsense. She's probably fast asleep after that enormous meal.'

Melanie had never seen anything more enchanting as she stood beside Carlton on deck and watched the moonlight reflected on the calm sea, with the lights twinkling like diamonds along the coast.

'Have you enjoyed it all, Melanie?' Carlton asked.

'It's been the most exciting time in my whole life,' she confessed. 'If only my father had still been at home, working away on his violins, then life would just seem perfect at the moment.'

'I remember him as a very charming man, and I know Aunt Millicent thought he was rather . . . rather wonderful.'

'Yes, she told me,' said Melanie, softly.

'I know that he had a special feel for the violin, as an instrument, I mean. His work was always in great demand.'

'I have one he was specially proud of, besides an old one which belonged to my great-grandfather. There have been others in the family who were passionately fond of music, and my mother's father was quite well-known as a pianist. She loved the piano, but Father's favourite was always the violin.'

'Yes, I heard about your violins,' said Carlton, 'and a little about Jordan's. I always intended to visit Barholme and meet your father, but somehow it could never be arranged. I used to travel rather a lot, I'm afraid. What about the young man who is helping you, Melanie?'

'George? I'm afraid he's not a musician. He doesn't play any musical instrument.'

'I meant . . . is he really someone special for you? Are you . . . er . . . planning to marry him one day?'

'Well . . . ' She paused, wondering how to answer him.

'Please don't think I'm being inquisitive, and poking my nose into your private affairs, but it is rather important.'

'He has asked me to marry him, but I don't love him enough. The shop hasn't been doing too well, but I hope to take over the reins myself, and perhaps I could teach music to help out with income. I'm sure I could get quite a few pupils from Barholme and the surrounding area.'

'But, don't you think you might marry one day? I mean, you aren't an out and out career woman? You do believe in marriage, don't you?'

'If . . . if I loved someone, I would

145

like to get married,' she confessed, the warm colour in her cheeks.

'Then you're a perfectly sweet normal girl. I envy you. I was a normal man myself until . . . '

He rubbed his stiffened arm.

'You'll overcome that surely!'

He turned to look down at her, his eyes dark pools in the moonlight, then suddenly his good arm was around her and he was kissing her gently, then passionately.

'We should not have looked at the sea by moonlight, sweet Melanie,' he said, softly. 'It makes one forget.'

'Forget?'

'That life can be a bit of a mess.'

'But very exciting,' she said, her heart singing with happiness. It all seemed like a dream, and she would soon wake up, but it was something to remember for the future, whatever happened. These few moments would be precious to her for the rest of her life.

'You'd better take those spectacles back to Aunt Millicent. She'll wonder what has happened to you. We'll work again on my music as soon as we get back home. I can hear it all inside me, and I know it all now, almost note perfect, yet some adjustments will have to be made. I'm going to call it 'Enchanted Island'. It is romantic music, Melanie, and not the bitter sounds I began to make when I first knew that my arm was so badly injured. Aunt Millicent rescued me and bullied me into taking hold of myself, and . . . and she found you.'

Melanie had nothing to say. She wanted to tell him how happy she was, but no words would come. Then as they walked back towards her cabin, she began to feel that it was she who had been caught in some sort of enchantment. She had forgotten all about Marcia Dawson.

For a time all things had seemed possible between herself and Carlton, but it had only been the moonbeams shining on the sea. One could not catch a moonbeam.

7

The hotel in Athens, situated near the Plaka, was charming thought Melanie, when they arrived there the following day. Marcia made no secret of the fact that she was delighted to be on terra firma again, but Melanie felt that part of herself had been left behind on the ship. She had loved the cruise and thought that she would be happy to spend her life at sea!

'You would soon change your mind after a few storms,' said Miss Kendall. 'For my part, I'm going up to the rooftop terrace to relax and just look around. You can see the Acropolis from there.'

'And I'm going to enjoy that gorgeous blue bathroom,' Melanie said, smiling. 'Carlton wants to listen to bouzouki music. I think he wants me to take more dictation while everything is

148

fresh in his mind.'

Melanie could speak of Carlton much more naturally now that he had kissed her in the moonlight. At one time her love for him had been tempered by awe, but now she could think of him with tenderness as well as love, feeling that they had shared some precious moments together.

Marcia had not been feeling too well, and began to complain of a stomach upset.

'You eat far too much, my dear,' Miss Kendall told her bluntly. 'Oh, I know you use it up in boundless energy, but the food *is* rather rich.'

'I've never had this trouble before,' said Marcia, crossly. 'Carlton and I were planning to go to a Night Club in the Plaka.'

'Well, I'll look after you and Melanie can go instead,' said Miss Kendall, kindly. 'I've got a stomach settler which I can give you, and you'll soon feel better. Perhaps you've picked up a small virus.'

Marcia looked far from pleased about the solicitous care which Miss Kendall offered, though she agreed to try the stomach settler.

'It might clear up the trouble, then I can go to the Plaka. It would be a bore for Carlton if he's stuck with his little secretary girl instead of me for the whole evening.'

Melanie's pleasure faded a little. Marcia never failed to remind her of her place. Carlton and Bert Sloan had gone to the swimming pool since Bert considered that it might be good therapy for Carlton's arm, and the three women were sitting in the lounge area of the foyer.

'We will all go up to my bedroom,' Miss Kendall decided, 'and we can sit out on the terrace if you don't feel like going up to the roof, Marcia.'

'I feel like lying down on my bed,' Marcia confessed. 'Perhaps I ought to see a doctor. Perhaps Carl could arrange that for me.'

'I will inform the courier,' said Miss

Kendall. 'You must certainly go to bed and we'll send for a doctor if you feel so ill.'

'No, I may be okay after your medicine has time to take effect,' said Marcia, hastily.

'Can I do anything to help?' Melanie offered.

'Certainly not,' said Marcia, crossly. 'I don't want you flapping round.'

'Quite right,' said Miss Kendall rather swiftly. 'I'm much more competent to deal with this than you.'

In the end Marcia had to rest, and Miss Kendall insisted on looking after her while Carlton took Melanie on a tour of Athens.

'I know it quite well,' said Miss Kendall, 'and so does Marcia, but it's all new to you, my dear, and it will be new to Carlton when he sees it again through your eyes.'

'Well . . .' Melanie hesitated as Carlton came up to them, his face glowing with health.

'Of course I'll take Melanie,' he

assured his Aunt Millicent, 'though she must bring her notebook. This time I really do want to work.'

He went along to Marcia's room to commiserate with her, but Marcia was in no mood to be cheered up. She felt rotten, and she was angry and frustrated at being left out of things. The doctor had been called, and had diagnosed indigestion, and Marcia was sure to feel better after her medicine had taken effect.

'I'll probably be perfectly fit in another hour,' she said. 'Why can't you come back early and we'll listen to bouzouki music together?'

'Because you're better to have complete rest,' said Carlton, 'and not risk doing any damage. You must keep well for the sake of your tour.'

'That's true,' Marcia agreed, 'though I've never had a stomach upset in the States.'

It was one of the most wonderful days Melanie had ever known, as she and Carlton explored the beautiful city which caught at her heart.

'I had not imagined that the Acropolis was so beautiful,' she said. 'I mean, one sees pictures, but the reality is so much more wonderful.'

'Would you like to climb the hill and visit the Chapel of the Knights of St. John?' Carl asked, 'or would you like to go back to the hotel now, and get ready for the Plaka?'

Melanie considered for a moment. It was growing darker, but the hill fascinated her.

'I would like to see the Chapel,' she decided.

Together they climbed the many steps, then got into an incline train for the ride to the top.

The Chapel was tiny, but once again Melanie was enchanted by it, then Carlton put his good arm round her shoulders, pulling her to him as they gazed out on the wonderful panoramic view of the lights of Athens. Melanie felt that she had never been more happy in her life. It wouldn't last, she kept telling herself, but it was an experience which would enrich her life for always.

'We haven't really got very much work done with regard to your music,' she said, to Carlton, as they returned to the hotel.

'No,' he admitted, 'but you see, the fact that I now *want* to work is true progress. Melanie, I had planned to stay in London for a week or two, but now I think I would like to go back to Ardlui, my own home on the outskirts of Edinburgh. Aunt Millicent keeps house for me, as you know, and we both love it there. It is quiet and peaceful, with a lovely view of the Firth of Forth. Would you be willing to come home with me and get down to really serious work? What about your own business? Could you still leave it for a little while longer?'

'Well . . . ' Melanie thought for a long moment, 'I would have to see how it is faring, of course.'

It would all have to end one day, then she would have to go home, and she wanted her independence. She could never marry George now that she knew what love was really like, so she would have to concentrate on finding as many pupils as possible, and in trying to run Jordan's efficiently. Yet it was tempting to stay with Carl for a little longer.

'Jane Price is looking after it all for you, isn't she?' asked Carl. 'Well, she's got a wide experience in that sort of thing. She used to work for William Scott, one of the best known names in London. Your father probably knew the firm, or knew of them.'

'You know Mrs. Price well . . . and Shelley?' she asked, casually.

He nodded. 'And Shelley,' he agreed.

'She's . . . she's a very beautiful girl, isn't she?'

'Yes.'

Melanie knew Carlton well enough now to read the signs and he did not want to talk about Shelley Price. He could retreat into himself so quickly, she thought.

'Jane Price will have Jordan's running

like clockwork,' said Carlton, 'so I don't think you need worry about it unduly. What about it, Melanie?'

The thought of going to Ardlui was becoming more and more attractive, and she found herself accepting Carlton's invitation, come what may.

'I would love to work with you until your suite of music is finished,' she admitted. 'All right, I'll be delighted to come, Carlton, if Miss Kendall has no objections.'

'You know jolly fine she has none,' he laughed. 'It was her idea in the first place.'

Then his eyes sobered and he reached out a finger to pull one of her chestnut curls.

'Now it is my idea, Melanie.'

'So you two have found your way back!'

Melanie's heart leapt as Marcia's ringing voice came from the end of the corridor where they were standing, and slowly the older girl began to saunter towards them. She certainly looked as though she had recovered very well from her attack of indigestion.

'I'd better go and change,' said Melanie looking at the other girl's sheer elegance.

'No hurry, my dear. Miss Kendall's elixir is sheer magic. It had me right as rain in no time, and I can't be too grateful to her. Now I think I would like to come to the Plaka after all, Carl.'

'I've invited Melanie,' said Carlton, quietly. 'The arrangements have already been made.'

'Oh no, it's quite all right,' said Melanie, hastily. 'I don't mind if . . . if you two want to go.'

She could see the thunder clouds gathering on his face again. Carlton hated women squabbling over him. For a moment she was tempted to suggest that they could all go, then she knew she would feel out of everything if she tagged along with him and Marcia.

'I . . . I'm rather tired after that long walk up the hill to see the tiny Chapel.'

'All this sight-seeing!' said Marcia,

indulgently, though Melanie could see that she was determined to have Carlton to herself this evening.

'Miss Kendall is preparing for her departure to Istanbul,' said Marcia, in response to Carlton's query as to where she was. 'She has Bert Sloan helping her to pack all the purchases she has made, into her cases. Miss Kendall is rather a messy traveller. I would have thought that part of your job would be helping her to keep her belongings tidy, Melanie.'

'Oh dear, maybe I'd better help then,' she said, 'if you'll excuse me.'

Carlton said nothing, but she could see the anger still in his eyes as he turned to look at her. Marcia seemed to remind him constantly of his stiffened arm since she was given to stroking him gently. Already, though, it was a great deal better, and one day he may regain the complete use of it. Perhaps, then, he would only remember all that Marcia had been to him over the years.

Even if he found Shelley Price's

dazzling looks irresistible, and Melanie's knowledge of music helpful when he wanted to compose his music, he would always want to return to Marcia Dawson. Melanie felt that they were bound together. She was just another girl in Carl's life, and she didn't count.

'I suppose you spent the afternoon getting your music down on manuscript,' she heard Marcia saying, lightly, as she turned away.

'Not yet, but I'm making progress . . .'

Carlton's voice faded as Melanie reached her bedroom. The excitement of the day seemed to have evaporated, leaving her tired with her nerves rather on edge. She found Miss Kendall surrounded by a sea of small packages, while she offered Bert advice which was spoilt when she changed her mind every five minutes. Bert's eyes were turned up to the ceiling.

'Miss Kendall, we'll never get through Customs at this rate,' he protested.

'Nonsense. It's all cheap stuff and not on the list of forbidden items. It just takes a little ingenuity. Melanie will work it out, won't you, dear? Now, let's see . . . where can I put this little donkey, and this print which I shall have framed for my bedroom. I shall want to buy Turkish Delight in Istanbul. I adore Turkish Delight.'

'Well at least you can eat that, Miss Kendall,' said Bert, tiredly, after he and Melanie had brought order to the chaos.

'Did you and Carlton have a happy time, dear?' asked Miss Kendall, ignoring him.

'It was wonderful,' said Melanie. 'I've never seen such views. It's something I shall remember always.'

'Are you now going to the Plaka? What will you wear? It must be something very nice.'

'I'm not going. Marcia and Carlton are going, so I thought I had better stay here.'

Miss Kendall frowned. 'But why? Stupid girl. You are too young to stay in with an old woman like me. One must enjoy life while one is young, my dear.'

Melanie thought Miss Jordan was enjoying life quite well, even if she was no longer quite so young.

'Last time I was in Istanbul, I went to a Night Club and took pictures of the belly dancers,' she informed them. 'One would expect them all to be very slender with all that rolling about, but they were really quite plump. I don't find the human body particularly attractive when such a lot of flesh is exposed. Now, Bert, I want to see the new bridge which joins Europe and Asia and I would like to take a photograph of it, so see that my camera is handy.'

Bert was about to say something, then he changed his mind, though Melanie saw that his eyes were twinkling with suppressed laughter.

'You also took a great many pictures of a Turkish guide,' he teased.

'I know. He looked like Omar Sharif,' Miss Kendall grinned. 'The human body can be very attractive in some men.'

161

'Carlton would like me to come to Ardlui for a week or two when we return home,' said Melanie, feeling that she wanted to know if Miss Kendall really was in favour of this idea. 'I think he is now absorbing all sorts of impressions, and could really get down to work when he returns home.'

The older woman brightened considerably.

'Splendid! That's a great idea. I feel that Carl has it in him to do some very fine work, and you can help him, Melanie. Even if it means putting his wishes before your own, I really feel that this is very important, my dear. You can be so helpful to him.'

'I'm glad you approve of the idea,' said Melanie, sincerely.

'Come on then, dear. Let's all go to the dining room and find something nice to eat. All of a sudden I have quite a big appetite.'

8

Melanie stepped aboard the plane for the return flight to London with no small regret, yet the future looked bright with promise. She had grown to love this ancient part of the world and she was taking back many glorious memories of wonderful scenery, marvellous old buildings, fun, laughter, narrow streets, traffic jams and a lovely shopping spree in the flea market.

Miss Kendall, Carlton and she were due to go back to the hotel in London before travelling to Scotland, and they said goodbye to Marcia at the Airport.

'After my tour of the States, I am going to do the provinces,' she told Carlton, 'but I'll be back to see you before I leave for New York. You know, I don't think you're exercising that arm enough. It's really time it was back to normal now, Carl. Don't you think you ought to get another opinion? I'm sure that lots more could be done.'

Carlton said nothing, but Melanie heard Miss Kendall muttering under her breath.

'And I hope that little store of yours becomes quite successful, Melanie,' went on Marcia, kindly. 'I expect this holiday will have been the highlight of your existence. It will be something to tell your grandchildren, my dear.'

Melanie caught Carlton's eye, and he shook his head slightly. Apparently he had not mentioned that Melanie was going back to Edinburgh with him and Miss Kendall.

Marcia's tone was so patronizing that Melanie decided to say nothing either. She bade the other girl a formal goodbye, feeling that she was unlikely to meet her again. Nor would she break her heart over that. She would listen to that wonderful voice on records, Melanie decided, and try to remember that artists of her quality were inclined to be temperamental.

Melanie was happy to be in London again, and she would like to have stayed longer. The holiday had enriched her life, but seeing the busy London streets again caught at her heart. It was like nowhere else in the whole world, she decided.

The following morning a taxi took all of them to the railway station, and soon they were on the Edinburgh train. Bert Sloan had seen to most of the baggage, and during the journey north, he made Carlton do exercises with a soft ball, squeezing and unsqueezing the fingers.

'You're improving,' Bert said, rather excitedly. 'I do think it's a lot better, Mr. Kendall.'

'It's no such thing!' said Carlton. 'It's as stiff as ever. I can hardly hold the ball.'

'Bert is right,' said Miss Kendall. 'I remember, if you don't, Carl, that at one time you couldn't even hold the ball. Now your hand is much more supple.'

'But my arm is still completely stiff.'

It was the first time he had discussed his accident at length in front of Melanie. At one time he had seemed to hide it away from her, but now he seemed to accept her as part of his entourage, she thought with a slight smile. Sometimes she even wondered if he was beginning to take her for granted!

The previous evening, at Miss Kendall's prompting, she had rung up Mrs. Price at the flat above Jordan's.

'So you're home, Miss Jordan!' the older woman said, and there was a faint trace of reserve in her voice.

'Yes, Mrs. Price. Is everything all right?'

'Everything is splendid. I've kept it all well up to date, and I'll be able to hand over to you whenever you like.'

'That's what I'm ringing up about,' Melanie told her. 'I may have to go on to Edinburgh for a week or two to stay at Ardlui, and help Mr. Kendall until . . . well . . . until he has finished all the work he plans to do. Would you consider staying on for another week or two?'

Mrs. Price's reserve vanished instantly, and Melanie suspected that it had been mainly due to the older woman's insecurity. So far she did not appear to have found a home for herself and her daughter, nor had Miss Kendall been able to 'look around' before she went to Greece.

'That would be splendid,' Mrs. Price said, thankfully. 'We'd love to stay on, Shelley and I. We're rather enjoying it here. We've found lots of old stock which we've cleaned up, and it has been selling like hot cakes. We'll really have to talk about this angle when I see you again, Miss Jordan. It's wonderful what sort of things are in demand these days.'

'That sounds very promising,' Melanie told her, laughing. 'I'm not surprised about the old stock. I've been meaning to tidy up for ages.'

'Well, it's been fun doing it for you. I've kept some things back, too. I think we can get a very good price for them, if we go about it carefully.'

'I shall leave that to you then,' said Melanie. 'I'll come and see you as soon as I can.'

Melanie was thinking about the telephone conversation as she lay back against the cushions, as the train carried her swiftly and smoothly towards Edinburgh. Miss Kendall had not yet had time to find the promised accommodation for Mrs. Price, and no doubt the woman had been searching on her own behalf. But houses were not easy to come by even in quiet towns like Barholme, and she must have been unsuccessful because of the heartfelt relief which was in her voice when Melanie asked her to stay on.

But suppose there was nowhere for her to go by the time Melanie's own job ended. What would happen then? That problem was like a tiny cloud looming up on the horizon, and as the days passed, it was likely to grow much bigger ... unless it was resolved. Melanie's thoughts grew jumbled then were lulled by the rhythm of the train wheels, and she slept.

★   ★   ★

Melanie loved Ardlui, the charming detached house on the outskirts of Edinburgh, even if the wind had a sudden bite, and she was glad she had one or two sweaters in her luggage. If the weather grew cooler, she would have to go to Barholme soon and pick up some of her warmer clothing.

Carlton's housekeeper, Mrs. McAndrew, welcomed them home gravely, but Melanie could see the delight in her eyes and the eager way she fussed over Carlton and Miss Kendall.

'This is Miss Jordan,' Miss Kendall introduced, 'Alexander Jordan's daughter.'

'How do you do, Miss,' said Mrs. McAndrew with deference. 'I remember your father well. He used to come here in the old Master's time, when I was just a young housemaid.'

'Different world in those days,' Miss Kendall said rather gruffly. 'Did you get the message to prepare a bedroom for Miss Jordan?'

'Oh yes, indeed. It's all ready.'

She showed Melanie up to the small but comfortable bedroom set aside for her.

'If you need anything I've overlooked, Miss, don't be afraid to ask,' she told Melanie, formally, though there was a hint of curiosity in her glance. It seemed that Carlton had not fully explained her position in the household.

'It all looks charming, thank you, Mrs. McAndrew,' she said. 'I'll be very comfortable here, I'm sure.'

Mrs. McAndrew had pulled the curtains.

'Mr. Carlton usually prefers a wee bit of supper after a journey, but if you want anything more than that, then I'll be most happy . . . '

'I'm sure it will be quite enough for me,' said Melanie, smiling. 'I'll have a wash, if I may, then come straight down again.'

'It's a casserole, so it won't spoil, my dear. I wasn't sure of the time you'd arrive. You'll find plenty of extra towels in this airing cupboard, and I've found you some nice scented soap. Miss Kendall keeps buying it, then she declares it's much too fancy for her.'

Melanie laughed. 'I've got my own toilet things, but I love nice soap.' She hesitated for a moment, then she smiled. 'I've come here to work, Mrs. McAndrew, and to help Mr. Carlton with his music, so I might be using up some of that pretty soap while I'm here.'

The older woman's eyes crinkled. 'It will be a pleasure to have Mr. Carlton working again,' she said, softly. 'It will be a real pleasure.'

The holiday seemed to have put new life into Carlton because the pattern set for each day was a busy one. He went for a brisk walk in the early morning, and sometimes he encouraged Melanie to walk with him.

'It clears the cobwebs,' he explained, 'and Bert says that I must progress to jogging very soon. But I don't care for jogging. I like to see things as I walk along, so that each moment can be packed full of interest. With jogging I just have to endure it until I return home, and I feel that my precious time has been wasted.'

'Not if it gets you better,' she protested.

'What's the use of having large leg muscles, and none at all on my arm?' he demanded, and she said no more. But if he didn't keep at those exercises, she might be tempted to say a great deal more, thought Melanie. He was far too sorry for himself at times.

The mornings were spent in dictating the music for her to write in manuscript form, and gradually they were beginning to work together very well. Carlton worked hard, altering and re-arranging until he was satisfied with the result, and Melanie had to follow him, swiftly and competently to capture the flow of composition. The fact that they had so recently visited all the places which had inspired the music helped enormously, and somehow this suite of music seemed to capture all the magic of the Greek Islands for her. She had held her temper, too, when he had practically pushed her off the piano stool, and had tried to play over several notes to her to explain the effect he wanted to create. For a brief moment he had been able to use his fingers, then he had caught at his arm and the fingers had curled tightly, so that she knew he was in pain. He had muttered under his breath, and had asked her to sit down again, but this time she had played over the music, note perfect, and once again they carried on with the work.

In a strange way she grew more shy of Carlton now that she realized the measure of his talent, and her love for him was enhanced by great admiration and respect. He might be a very great man one day, and she had no right in longing to be the most important woman in his life. He was entitled to anything she could give him, without her demanding an equal amount in return.

'You're very quiet,' he said to her one evening after they had spent an exhausting day over the slow movement of the music, and were now walking in the fresh air.

'I can still hear your melody in my head,' she said. 'I'm listening to it.'

'Really?' he asked, pleased. 'Can you really follow it in your head? That's very good. It means that it should have appeal, for a few people, anyway.'

'I think it will have enormous appeal,' she told him, 'especially if it is included in the programme for the Promenade Concerts.'

Carlton's smile slowly faded and he went to stand with his elbows on a gate by the roadside, leaning over into the field.

'It looks like Winter,' he said. 'Nothing is growing. Everything seems

174

to have died, even that long grass. The trees are bare, and the countryside looks dull.'

'It's only sleeping,' she said. 'It will all be up again in Spring. We all have Winters in our lives, but if we have patience, then we can look forward to Spring-time. That's a wonderful time of year.'

'I know what you're trying to say,' he told her, 'but it doesn't help. I miss it all like Hell.'

'I'm sure you must do,' she said, gently. 'I wonder how Miss Dawson's tour of America has been received. It should be finished by now.'

'Oh, Marcia always lands on her feet,' said Carlton, turning away. 'Do you like it here, Melanie? Do you like Ardlui?'

'It's the nicest house I've ever seen,' she said, honestly. 'It's so bright and cheerful as well as comfortable and Mrs. McAndrew seems to run things so competently. But old houses like Ardlui have to grow. It's only generations of loving care which give them that sort of patina. It just can't be matched any other way. And Miss Kendall has been busy helping in the garden. I saw her from my bedroom window this morning.'

To her delight, she had found that her bedroom window overlooked the back garden, beyond which was a panoramic view of the Firth of Forth. Melanie loved her room, but once again she had the feeling that she was much too happy. Something was bound to happen. Her life seemed to be like a beautiful bubble from Miss Kendall's expensive soap and, she feared it was going to burst all too soon.

Carlton reached out and pulled her close and kissed her tenderly.

'I'm beginning to love you very much, Melanie,' he told her. 'Did you know that?'

Her eyes filled with tears as she turned to look at him.

'Oh, Carlton . . . I don't know what to say. Do you really mean that?'

'Of course I mean it.'

He turned away, throwing out his hand with an air of frustration.

'Why didn't Aunt Millicent bring you home a year ago? Why is it always too late?'

'Too late?' She stared at him, bewildered.

'There are certain things I just can't do,' he said, quietly, 'and one of them is to take advantage of a young girl I've grown to like and admire, as well as love.'

He spoke in riddles, thought Melanie, puzzled. How could he be taking advantage of her? He had everything to give, but she had nothing in return, except her deep abiding love. But surely that was something worthwhile. If he really loved her, she would devote her whole life to his happiness.

'But Carlton . . .'

'I think we're going to be caught in the rain if we don't hurry,' he told her, shortly. 'Come on, Melanie, let's run for home.'

9

Melanie decided that she would go back to Barholme the following Sunday to pick up some of her warmer clothing. She had now been at Ardlui for several weeks and the weather had grown colder. She wondered for how much longer she would be required to stay, but when she asked Carlton, he was inclined to answer evasively. He was due to pay another visit to the specialist in London, and Melanie could see the signs of strain in him again.

'Sometimes I'm afraid of what he will tell me,' he confided, massaging his fingers as Bert Sloan had taught him to do each day. 'Sometimes I feel I must accept what has happened, and come to terms with myself. Then I feel that I just cannot accept it, and I want to lash out at . . . at whoever is nearest . . . and perhaps the one who is dearest to me. I'm poor company at the moment, my dear.'

'Then composing music is not enough for you?' she asked.

He rumpled his hair. 'How can it be! I don't know how good I am.'

'But it's such wonderful music!'

'You are prejudiced, you and Aunt Millicent because you know me and you are trying to encourage me. You also make allowances for my disability, even though you might not think so. You're probably completely unaware of feeling that way. But suppose I have arranged my music for full orchestra and it has to stand on its own merit. What then? Who would take the chance on playing the slow movement written for violin and orchestra, and give it that extra magic which comes from having a real *feel* for the music . . . something which is not there, on the manuscript, but which comes from the desire and enthusiasm to bring it all to life. I could have done it myself at one time. I want

179

people to listen to it, as I can hear it myself. You know for many years Souza was the only one who could conduct his famous music as *he* meant it to be heard. Perhaps mine is not important enough, but I would like people to hear it, as *I* want them to hear it.'

He stopped for a long moment, then smiled ruefully at Melanie.

'Sorry, my dear. I'm talking rubbish. Pay no attention to me.'

'No . . . no, I think I know what you mean,' she told him. 'I think, too, that you had better see that specialist. It's no use hiding from life and from disappointment and even tragedy. These things happen and we must make the best of them.'

He was looking at her blankly, but she felt that his thoughts were miles away.

'You're right, of course. I'll go with good heart and if the news is better than I fear . . . Melanie, we'll talk again, won't we?'

'Of course we will,' she assured him,

then as he shook his head and smiled, she wondered just what he'd had in mind.

Miss Kendall came in from the garden, her cheeks scarlet with her exertions. She had been sweeping up leaves and burning them on a huge bonfire, and her hair was perfumed with wood smoke.

'Samuel Templeton is a fool, Carl,' she said, clearly. 'He wants all his own way in that garden, and he's so cantakerous these days that I long to poke him with the hoe. He knows nothing about pruning. I have to watch him every second, and he called me an interfering old hen.'

'He's looked after the garden for a long time, Aunt Millicent.'

'Yes, too long,' said Miss Kendall, darkly. 'He ought to be retired, the silly old man. What have you two been doing? How is the music going, Carl?'

'Quite well,' he said, briefly.

Mrs. McAndrew came in to serve tea in the lounge, and she built up the cheerful fire against another crop of biting winds.

'I thought I had better go home to Barholme to collect more clothes, if I'm going to be here much longer,' said Melanie. 'I think I ought to see how Mrs. Price and Shelley are faring, too.'

Miss Kendall and Carlton exchanged glances.

'So you haven't discussed any future plans with Melanie, dear,' said Miss Kendall.

'No,' said Carlton, rather shortly.

'Well, it might be a good idea, then ... That sounds like a car. Are we expecting anyone this afternoon? It sounds as though we must be having a visitor,' she ended as wheels crunched on the gravel. 'Mrs. McAndrew has no cucumber left. I should like the last one, if you two have no objections.'

Melanie merely shook her head. Her quick ear had caught the strident tones she knew only too well, and a moment later the door flew open and Marcia Dawson walked in. She looked like an exotic parrot who had hopped into the canary's cage. Mrs. McAndrew was bringing up the rear, but Marcia was waving her away.

'I know where to go,' she said. 'So here you all are.'

She hurried forward to kiss Carlton, then Miss Kendall, though it was to Melanie that she turned.

'I've been wondering what happened to you, Miss Jordon. I've been to see your little shop at Barholme and there was Jane Price, and Shelley, all busy selling mouth organs. Jane said you were still here, though I found that very hard to believe. Surely the holiday was over long ago? You must really be trying to take the last out of it, my dear.'

'Do sit down, Marcia,' said Miss Kendall, pointing to a chair. 'I'm sure Mrs. McAndrew will cut some more sandwiches. You are a long way north, unless you're doing a tour of Scotland? How did you fare in America?'

'Quite delightful, as always,' said Marcia, accepting a cup of tea, 'though tragedy has struck over the provinces tour. I shall tell you all about it in a moment. Do you think Mrs. McAndrew could find me some good beef, or ham? Chicken would do. I really am famished, Carl darling. I came straight here by taxi from the station, but I must be on the night train for London. I know it's disappointing, but we'll just have to catch up with our news.'

'What sort of tragedy?' asked Miss Kendall, her interest aroused.

'In a moment,' said Marcia, her eyes growing calculating as she stared at Melanie.

'Are you still the little secretary, my dear, and helping Carl with writing down his compositions?'

'We've been working very hard,' said Melanie, crisply. Something about Marcia Dawson always caught her on the raw, and she could feel her temper stirring.

'That's splendid. Then my journey has not been wasted, has it? I just didn't know what to do when Willy . . . my

184

accompanist, you know . . . when Willy got ill. Now it's going to mean an operation. The poor man has been brewing up an ulcer, apparently, and he's had to go into hospital. But I'm due to leave for Manchester on Monday, and there's just no time at all.'

'For what?' asked Miss Kendall.

'To find an accompanist, of course. I mean, I can't cancel because the publicity would be bad, yet how can I give of my best if I can't find anyone to play for me . . . someone *I* can work with . . . someone . . . '

She stared at Melanie.

'You could do it, Melanie. You aren't particularly *good*, of course, but neither are you as bad as *some* accompanists. They are all out to give a solo performance with no consideration for the singer. You could come home with me now, to London, and we could have a few days practice before leaving for Manchester. It would be a marvellous opportunity for you. Who knows but you might not build yourself a worthwhile career so that you don't have to serve behind the counter, or teach stupid children. Sometimes parents decide to have their children taught when they have no aptitude for music whatsoever. They are tone deaf. That makes it very hard for the poor teacher, and you'd really do much better as an accompanist. If you do well for me, I shall recommend you after I get Willy back again.'

Melanie hardly knew what to say, but her every instinct was against taking up Marcia's offer.

'Well, I doubt if I can do that,' she said, and turned to look at Carlton whose face had gone wooden. 'And besides, I don't agree with you that I may be teaching stupid children. Children are not stupid, and most musicians start their training . . . '

'Oh, don't be so literal, Melanie darling,' Marcia interrupted. 'You know very well what I mean.'

'I . . . I've promised to stay here in

Edinburgh to finish my work for Carlton,' Melanie said.

'That, surely, is something which could be postponed quite easily,' said Marcia, airily. 'Carlton has no schedule to keep. I have.'

'If Melanie doesn't want to play for you, then I don't see why you should bully her, Marcia,' said Miss Kendall, pouring out another cup of tea. 'It is nonsense to say you can't find anyone else. There must be a great many young people who would jump at the chance.'

Marcia's eyes began to sparkle.

'I want this girl.'

'So do I,' said Carlton, quietly. 'I know you, Marcia, and you would bully Melanie unmercifully. You're like a tigress when you're on tour . . . it goes with that voice of yours and we are all willing to forgive you because of the beauty and pleasure you bring to so many people, but Aunt Millicent is quite right. Find someone else, my dear.'

Marcia's cheeks had flushed. She

enjoyed Carlton's praise for her voice, but she hated to be thwarted over Melanie.

'What reason did you give our little friend here for wanting to keep her?' she asked. 'Is she such a genius at writing out your dictation? Or are you trying to make her fall for you? Not that you'll have to try very hard. I think she was infatuated from the very beginning, and with a little bit of flattery . . .'

'That's enough!' said Carlton. 'Anything between Melanie and myself is our own affair. It has nothing to do with you.'

'Oh, hasn't it?' asked Marcia, 'and I'm not talking about what is between us, Carl, and what has been between us. It will always be there, you know. You can't escape it, no matter how hard you try. But I'm talking about your trying to take advantage of a young girl.'

'Really!' cried Melanie. 'Really, you shouldn't say such things. I'm not so very young, and no one has tried to take advantage of me, nor would I allow it.'

'But what if you didn't *know* about it?' asked Marcia, gently. 'I don't suppose they'll have told you they intend to sell your precious violin for you. Or have they? Has it all been discussed between you, and am I quite wrong?'

'Don't listen to her malicious tongue, Melanie,' cried Miss Kendall, standing up. 'How dare you come out with such a statement when you know very well that . . . that it is all distorted.'

'Are you now telling me that you have never . . . *never* contemplated the idea of putting that violin up for sale at Sotherby's? Didn't you moot that idea in my hearing, and aren't you going to have Jane Price giving it a good examination while you've got Melanie Jordan here, well out of the way? Or hasn't she managed to examine it yet?'

Melanie began to feel sick with the shock of Marcia's words, as the place began to reel about her, even though the words did not make a great deal of sense. Her old violin!

'But . . . but why should they want to sell my old violin?' she asked. 'It's no Stradivarius.'

'No, but it's an Amati. Didn't you know that it could bring in many thousands of pounds? It's quite an event when one comes up for sale at Sotheby's. Jane Price can have a good look at it, and if it is as good as they think, you'll be persuaded to sell. After all, you have two violins, haven't you? You have one your father made, and it should be quite good enough for the sort of career you might have, since you seem to be bent on teaching. It's probably good enough, too, for orchestral work.'

She looked at Melanie who stared back, dumbly. She was trying desperately to assimilate all that Marcia was telling her.

'And Carlton needs money now, don't you, dear?' Marcia continued. 'He can no longer earn nice fat fees for orchestral conducting, or solo violin performances. He wants to compose, but it will take time to have his music recognized, and any income from that flowing in. I expect he's been leading up to a proposal. It won't seem like gold-digging, since you're hard up except for that violin, but if it brings in a nice round sum, why then, you're quite a catch, my dear. Isn't that how it goes, Carl?'

Carlton Kendall's face was chalk-white with his dark eyes blazing. Melanie could see that he was furiously angry.

Miss Kendall had pushed the tea trolley away, but for once she had not a word to say, then she moistened her lips.

'You should have been a barrister,' she said to Marcia. 'How you can twist things to your own ends. Melanie, my dear, if you would only consider Marcia Dawson for one moment . . .'

'I *have* got an old violin,' said Melanie, slowly, her eyes on Carlton, 'and Shelley Price asked for the key of the cupboard where I had locked it away. And you have examined the violin many times, Miss Kendall, and discussed it with my father, and Carlton . . . Carlton . . .'

She fought back the tears. He *had* kissed her, and he had been wooing her gently, knowing that that was the best way to make her respond. She had fallen in love with him. They had taken her on the cruise which was bound to stir her heart, then they had brought her home to this lovely old house which she could not help loving.

'Do you believe her?' Carlton was asking. 'Do you *really* believe her?'

'I . . . I don't know.'

Her eyes fell away from his as he reached over and put his hands on her shoulders, then he pushed her away, quite roughly.

'I see you do,' he said, harshly. 'It looks as though you've got yourself a pianist, Marcia. What a price you are willing to pay!'

Miss Kendall rose rather shakily.

'Melanie, I think we . . . we should have a little talk,' she began. 'I really think . . . '

'Oh, leave it, Aunt Millicent,' said Carlton, roughly. 'Can't you see she will believe what she *wants* to believe? It's always that way. People only ever believe what they want to believe.'

'But I only want to help,' Miss Kendall objected.

'Famous last words,' said Marcia, though she, too, was looking rather pale as her eyes followed Carlton. He had been staring out of the window, and now he turned and strode from the room.

'He's in the huff,' said Marcia, 'but he'll get over it. He always does.'

'This time you've gone too far, Marcia,' said Miss Kendall, quietly. 'If I can be glad about anything, it is that Carlton will be completely free of you from now on. I don't think you will ever be welcome in this house.'

'He'll *never* be free of me,' said

Marcia. 'You're both put out because I put a spoke in your little wheel, and when you both stop to consider it all a little longer, you will be grateful to me. No good would have come of it. You never know, the violin could be worthless after all, and Carlton could have committed himself to the child. Even I would be better value, though I can always see through him, and he doesn't like that, does he?'

'I think you'd better go, Marcia,' said Miss Kendall, and Melanie had never heard her voice more icy.

Marcia shrugged and turned to her.

'What are you going to do, Melanie? I'm offering you a wonderful chance to come to London with me, then to do a tour of the provinces. Who knows we may even go back to the United States? There was some talk of that before I left. Wouldn't you like to travel with me? It can be even more rewarding than going on a cruise. In fact, it could be the start of a new career for you, and there's nothing much wrong with a girl having her own career. But we haven't much time, you know. The taxi is due back in another fifteen minutes, so go and pack your stuff. You'll have to get used to packing quickly and efficiently, if you're going to travel with me . . . '

'I wouldn't dream of it!' broke in Melanie, choking back her tears. 'I don't want to be your accompanist, and I don't want to go to London with you, or to Manchester, or to the States or . . . or anywhere.'

'That's my girl,' said Miss Kendall, beaming with approval. 'Just wait till we tell Carlton your decision.'

'Neither am I staying here,' said Melanie, clearly. 'I . . . I don't want to hear any more. I'm leaving, too, but I'm going home to Barholme.'

10

Melanie felt that her limbs were like lead as she tried to pack her clothes. The taxi had come for Marcia Dawson, and the older girl had gone off in high dudgeon, unable to believe that Melanie had turned down this wonderful offer. After the taxi door slammed, Miss Kendall, looking rather cold and remote, climbed the stairs to Melanie's room.

'I've no intention of keeping you here against your will, my dear,' she said, 'but you are young and I feel responsible for you. I only ask that you leave in the morning instead of tonight. Bert Sloan will drive you to Barholme. I'm sure you won't want to leave your luggage here . . . ?'

'No,' said Melanie, huskily. 'I would prefer to take everything with me, and make a clean break. I . . . thank you for having me for one more night, since it is rather late. Miss Dawson was taking a sleeper to London, but there might be no trains to Barholme.'

'The decision to go is yours, not mine. I only hope you won't regret it, Melanie. I must say I feel very disappointed that you have met Marcia and that you were in close contact with her for several weeks, yet you seem unable to assess her character, and to judge the sort of person she is. Innocence is nice, but such naïvety is a bore. I see now I have made a mistake and that you are really much better to settle down in Barholme, and find yourself a few young pupils. You will probably make an excellent teacher, and will enjoy it after a while, but you are really not cut out for . . . for what I had in mind.'

She went out and closed the door, and Melanie felt as though something lovely and delicate as a piece of fragile porcelain had suddenly been broken. It was trust, she thought. It was delicate trust which had been broken between them. She had shown all too clearly that she could no longer trust Carlton, or Miss Kendall for that matter, and now she didn't know whether she had been right, or wrong. Miss Kendall had said she ought to be suspicious of Marcia and Marcia had thrown doubt on Carlton's motives. Who could she believe?

Was the violin *really* so valuable, she wondered? She could not even think of selling it, so she was unlikely to find out. What had made Miss Kendall imagine that she would be persuaded to sell it? It was a family possession, to be handed on to her children and grandchildren. Miss Kendall could not know how she would feel about such a thing; as though she would be breaking faith with her father if she allowed the violin to be sold out of the family. It meant more to her than it could possibly mean to anyone else.

And Carlton? Was he really depending on her to help him with finances?

Surely, if he needed a wife with money, there were plenty of other girls he could marry. Marcia, herself, for instance, though Marcia had said she could always see through him. Melanie also had a shrewd suspicion that Marcia was inclined to spend all she earned! She had made recordings, of course, but they were not so widely popular, nor had they such large sales as pop records. But Marcia's voice would still be heard when a lot of pop stars had come and gone. Her records would sell for very much longer.

Sadly she crawled into bed, the silence of the house rather weird and unnatural. Normally it was a cheerful place, with an occasional burst of song or a cheerful whistle to show that the people living under its roof were happy and contented with life. But now the atmosphere seemed heavy with brooding silence. The joy had gone out of the place.

In the early hours Melanie was still thinking over Marcia's words, and wondering if they were not too ridiculous even to consider. How could Miss Kendall be sure that her violin was so valuable? And why should she think Melanie would ever agree to sell it? The thoughts went round in her mind in ever repeating circles.

It was surely a fantastic reason for Carlton to want to marry her, though in fact, he had allowed her to think he loved her, but he had not proposed marriage. Could it be that Miss Kendall had bullied him into proposing to Melanie, but when it came to the crunch, he just could not do it?

Melanie's cheeks grew warm at the thought and the slow tears began to well in her eyes, and to run down her cheeks unchecked. She remembered how frank the older woman had been about wanting Carl to be happy, and how much it would please her if they fell in love, rather than allow Marcia to rule his life. She had arranged the cruise, hoping that something of this kind would come from it.

And Carlton had played up, as far as he was able. But would he have even *noticed* her if his arm had not been injured and he had still been absorbed in his career? Melanie remembered their first meeting, and bit her lip. He had been a vastly different man then from the young man, in jeans and sweater, who had wrapped a scarf round her head, and made her walk briskly up the road to 'clear the cobwebs'. Melanie remembered the tender moments they had shared, and how close she had felt to him. Was he only pretending then?

Her thoughts turned to Shelley Price, and she remembered Marcia's snippet of information that Carlton was inclined to collect 'lame ducks', usually young girls who were down on their luck. Perhaps he was well practised in kindness and generosity to girls like herself.

Unable to sleep, Melanie switched on her bedside lamp and saw the small collection of 'treasures' waiting to be packed; her small souvenirs from the holiday in Greece. She would leave the gifts which Carl had given her, she thought proudly, then she picked them up, her tears falling on to the little charm he had bought. No, she would take it with her. Whatever had happened, even if she had been a fool to think he would ever really care for her, she would always remember the lovely enchanted islands.

★ ★ ★

Next morning there was no sign of Carlton when Melanie walked downstairs carrying her cases. Mrs. McAndrew looked at her anxiously, but she treated Melanie with her usual warmth and kindness.

'I believe you're going home today, Miss Melanie,' she said. 'Miss Kendall says you've finished your work here now.'

'That's right, Mrs. McAndrew,' said Melanie, quietly. 'It's time I was back in Barholme. I've been away far too long.'

Rather shyly she handed Mrs. McAndrew a small gift-wrapped parcel. She had been shopping in Edinburgh one day and had seen a pretty piece of Celtic jewellery. It was a brooch made of silver, set with polished stones, and she had thought it would make a lovely gift for Mrs. McAndrew when the time came for her to return home. Now the time had come, and she watched as the older woman opened up her gift.

'My word, Miss Melanie, this is beautiful,' she said. 'There was no need, no need at all, but just the same I'm very pleased with it. I've often admired brooches of this kind, but I never thought I would own one. I . . . I just don't know how to say 'Thank you'.'

'No need for thanks, Mrs. McAndrew,' said Melanie. 'I'm just glad that you like it.'

'I do, and if I may say so, it's been a real pleasure to have you here. I hope you'll be coming back again, often, because I haven't seen Mr. Carlton so bright and cheerful for a long time.'

Melanie did not reply. Was he bright and cheerful that morning, too; glad to be rid of her?

'Sloan says he is driving you home, but I've prepared a good breakfast for you. It isn't so very far to Barholme, we know, but you're better with something to eat. I like something on my stomach when I set out on a journey, and you won't want to start cooking the very minute you open your own door.'

'Just coffee and maybe a bit of toast, Mrs. McAndrew.'

'Och, you'll need more than that! I'm grilling a piece of bacon, and a tomato. And what about two nice eggs?'

'No thanks,' said Melanie, her stomach rebelling at the thought of food. She was pale and heavy-eyed from sleeping badly, and she had a headache coming on.

'Very well then. Have a cup of coffee, then see how you feel. I'm glad we haven't got Miss Dawson staying again. She's an awful one to put up with, and she gets herself an appetite at quite the wrong times. Not that she's slow to eat at meal times either, and perhaps it's all that singing, but she's forever coming down to the kitchen, just to see what is in the fridge. Out she comes with a chicken leg, or a piece of sausage . . . Oh dear, there I go again. My tongue will trip me one of these days.'

The housekeeper's eyes were still anxious as they rested on the girl. Melanie certainly did not look as though she were ready for the journey home, and Mr. Carlton had come down very early and had gone out for his usual run without even drinking a cup of tea. They'd had a tiff, thought Mrs. McAndrew shrewdly. It was no doubt due to that Miss Dawson, since she had been doing a lot of talking when she arrived the previous afternoon. She had left in the evening, too, instead of staying as she usually did, and Mrs. McAndrew had breathed a sigh of relief. The girl never ceased to make mischief, even though it was a treat to hear her singing. Sometimes she sang an old Scots ballad, just for her, then Mrs. McAndrew felt she could forgive her anything, and it was then she could understand the bond between her and Mr. Carlton. They both had music in their souls.

Miss Kendall came downstairs as Melanie finished her coffee and toast. She looked at Melanie soberly, and her usually happy spirits were sadly lacking. Suddenly she looked rather old, thought Melanie, and a little bit tired. Perhaps she shouldn't be leaving her like this, but she would no doubt get short shrift if she offered to stay to look after Miss Kendall!

'So you're ready, my dear, and all packed. You're very efficient at that sort of thing, as I remember. I've seen Sloan, and he will bring the car round just as soon as he has checked it for oil and water.'

'Thank you,' said Melanie, quietly.

'I shall get in touch with Mrs. Price shortly, though you'll want to spend a few days together I've no doubt, sorting out any business problems and that sort of thing. I think Jane and Shelley had better come here, if Carlton has no objections until I can find her a permanent home. She has lost so many contacts by living abroad for such a long time, though I would not be surprised if she hasn't got a few irons in the fire herself. Jane . . . Mrs. Price . . . was always a very competent woman so you needn't feel that you are depriving her of a home. I'm sure she is grateful that she has been able to stay in the flat all this time. It must have helped her to get her bearings. We all need time to get our bearings, don't we?'

'Yes,' Melanie agreed, in a low voice. She was going to need a long time to get hers! Even now it seemed rather unreal that she was leaving Ardlui in such circumstances.

'I . . . I believe Mrs. Price used to be with a large firm of music sellers?' she said, after a long uncomfortable silence. The minutes, while she waited for Bert

Sloan seemed to be crawling past, and she had no wish to see Carlton again.

'Quite right. Jane has got experience in that line. If she had not been experienced, I might have considered things rather more deeply before leaving her in charge of Jordan's, but I knew she would manage everything for you very successfully. I would be very surprised if she has not been a great asset.'

'I'm sure everything will be in excellent order,' said Melanie.

Again there was a long silence, and she hardly knew what to say since she was finding conversation very difficult with Miss Kendall. She had the feeling that she had hurt the older woman very much. Should she confess that she was having second thoughts herself? In the cold light of day, she was beginning to remember that Marcia was not always to be trusted. Should she ask Miss Kendall to forgive her?

But for what? There was no doubt that Miss Kendall *had* been trying to manage her life for her. Nor had she denied Marcia's accusations in any way. That had weighed very deeply with Melanie, because she had seen from the older woman's face that there was truth in what Marcia was saying.

Suddenly she felt she had to know.

'Did you really consider selling my old violin?' she asked. 'Did you really discuss such a thing in front of Marcia?'

Miss Kendall faced her squarely.

'At one time, yes,' she said.

Melanie blinked. Miss Kendall was certainly honest.

'But not now?'

'It's the furthest thing from my thoughts. I wouldn't dream of it now. Ah, here's Bert Sloan. Well, goodbye, my dear. I'm sorry it has all turned out this way.'

Melanie swallowed a great lump which was rising in her throat.

'Goodbye, Miss Kendall. Thank . . . thank you for the lovely holiday and . . . and everything . . . ' she added, lamely. She wanted to say so much, but Miss Kendall was politely bowing herself out of her life.

She had a sudden aching longing to see Carlton again after all, but Bert Sloan was already loading her cases into the car. He opened the door and Melanie quietly climbed into the passenger seat. A moment later the car swung along the drive and out of the gates, turning left towards Barholme.

Melanie's heart was as heavy as lead, as she realised she might never see Ardlui again. Nor would she ever be really close to Carlton Kendall again either. She leaned back in her seat, fighting her tears as the familiar scenery whipped past. A very precious chapter of her life had just closed.

11

It was good to be back home, thought Melanie, as she climbed upstairs to the flat while Bert carried in her cases. But how small everything looked! Barholme, itself, had looked small, quiet and rather grey after Santorini, but Jordan's shop had seemed quite bright and spruce as Melanie got out of the car. Jane Price had certainly done a fine job in making the place look attractive, and the window display was so much smarter than it had ever been. Melanie had paused to look for a while before walking up the stairs to the flat.

Now Mrs. Price was hurrying towards her as she knocked on the door of the flat, then put her key in the lock before swinging open the door.

'Well, so you're home again, Miss Jordan!' she cried, warmly. 'I had planned such a celebration for you, but it has rather caught me on the hop. I did not expect such short notice . . . not that I need notice, of course,' she added, hurriedly.

'Yes, it was rather hurried,' Melanie agreed as she removed her coat. 'Sorry about that, but it was just how it happened.'

Shelley came running out of the bedroom, and Melanie was struck anew by the other girl's sheer loveliness. Shelley was now glowing with health and happiness.

'You . . . you look very well,' she commented, going forward to take the younger girl's hand.

'Well, it has been fun,' said Shelley. 'We've enjoyed it here a lot. I say, have you brought anything back from your cruise? I used to collect souvenirs when Daddy was in the Army, but we soon got fed up with being on the move all the time. It's nice to have souvenirs, though. Have you got anything interesting?'

'That will do, Shelley,' said her

mother, laughing a little. 'Please allow Melanie to get her breath back. She's only just walked in. I'm afraid we're inclined to think of you as a member of our family, my dear, since we have been living here. We see evidence of you all around, so you were always in our minds.'

'That's rather nice,' said Melanie, warmed in spite of herself. It was rather pleasant to have a welcome home instead of returning to an empty house.

Bert Sloan had stayed long enough to drink a cup of tea, then he, too, went quietly on his way and Melanie felt that one more link with Carlton had been broken. She had grown fond of Bert when they were all on the cruise, and she knew that he occupied a special place in the Ardlui household. Whether Carlton acknowledged it or not, Bert had done a great deal towards improving his arm.

'Would you like a meal now, or later,' Jane Price was asking.

'Later, please. At the moment I feel

that a warm bath and a clean change of clothing would do me more good.'

'I'll help you to unpack, if you like,' Shelley offered. 'I'm quite good at putting things away tidily.'

Melanie enjoyed being fussed over, and she was encouraged to sit in a warm dressing gown in front of a blazing fire while Mrs. Price and Shelley tidied away her clothes, then cooked a light, but satisfying meal.

'How is Carlton?' Shelley asked, eagerly. 'I do hope his arm is better now.'

'He's . . . ah . . . very well,' said Melanie, rather slowly. 'His arm is quite a lot better, but it still has a long way to go.'

'He's one of my favourite men. I adore him.'

Shelley's eyes were alight with fun mixed with warmth and affection, and Melanie could see why it would be difficult for any man to resist her.

'How is George?' she asked, thinking it would be quite nice to see him again, too. 'Have you seen much of him at all?'

This time Shelley's smile faded and her eyes grew wary. Melanie caught a meaningful glance passing between Mrs. Price and her daughter. It was the first sign of uneasiness she had detected, and her heart sank a little.

'He's very well, too,' said Shelley, carefully.

'Hasn't he been helping you?'

'Oh, yes, of course,' they both assured her, quickly.

Melanie said nothing. So George had not been at all nice to Mrs. Price and Shelley, she deduced, with a stab of irritation. Why did he have to be so small-minded? Why couldn't he have accepted that they were doing their best, and perhaps tried to help all he could instead of being obstructive?

The omelette which Mrs. Price had cooked was light and fluffy, and in spite of the depression which was beginning to set in, Melanie enjoyed it. She had eaten so little that morning, and she was beginning to feel tired after her restless night. The older woman watched the shadows on the young girl's face as she cleared away the tea table.

'I think you ought to go to bed for an hour or two, Melanie,' she suggested. 'You won't mind if I call you 'Melanie', will you?'

'No, I like it.'

'Well, what about it?'

'No, I'll just rest here,' Melanie told her. 'I'm feeling very comfortable, thanks to your kind ministrations.'

'Will you want to look at everything later?' Mrs. Price asked, diffidently.

'Gracious no, not until tomorrow.'

'Tell us about Greece then,' Shelley invited coming to sit on the carpet. She was like quicksilver, thought Melanie, as her mood changed from sunshine to shadows. She watched the firelight warming the girl's rounded cheeks and began to tell them about the cruise, without realising that her own face changed now and again as she recalled her visit to Santorini and the wonderful day she had spent there with Carlton.

'I think I will go to bed,' she said at length to Mrs. Price. 'I do feel rather tired.'

As she walked towards her bedroom, she could hear Shelley's clear voice, talking to her mother.

' . . . yes, but do you think she'll mind? I just don't know how she will feel . . . '

About what? wondered Melanie. About Jordan's? Did they have plans for the shop which might not meet with her approval? It was still her shop, thought Melanie, even if they had altered it quite a lot as though it were their own.

But it would all keep for another day, she thought tiredly. Tomorrow she would really begin to sort out her life once more, and to make plans for her own future.

★ ★ ★

Melanie was surprised by the improvements which Mrs. Price had made to the old shop, mainly because of the skill and ingenuity she had shown. With very little outlay, she had displayed the goods to the best advantage, and the whole place looked so much brighter and more welcoming.

'However did you manage such a miracle?' Melanie asked. 'I thought it looked marvellous when I stepped out of the car, but I didn't realize to what extent.'

'A few tins of paint and a jolly good look into your old stock,' the older woman laughed. 'Many things were becoming popular again, so I charged a proper price after cleaning them up properly, and I think you'll find that the books are encouraging.'

'I can't believe it,' said Melanie. 'I'm absolutely no good on retail. I'll have to earn my living by teaching, I'm afraid, and make a start by advertising for pupils.'

Remembering her plans, she glanced tentatively at Mrs. Price. There were several things she wanted to know, but she could sense a reserve in the older woman this morning, and Shelley, too, seemed to be avoiding her. Perhaps they were becoming concerned about their future.

'I'll have to go next door and say 'hello' to George,' she said. 'I've brought a few small gifts for the Aldridges, with a leather notecase for George. I thought he might like that.'

'He's in Glasgow at the moment,' said Shelley, quickly, 'on business for his father. He travels quite a lot for his own family business now.'

'Oh, I see,' said Melanie. So George was now taking a great deal more interest in the family firm. Perhaps that was all for the best.

Melanie remembered the last time she and George had spoken on the telephone, and she turned to look at Shelley speculatively, wondering afresh why she had wanted the key to her private cupboard.

'Oh, by the way . . . ' she began, then the telephone shrilled and Mrs. Price picked it up.

'Miss Jordan?' she asked. 'Yes, she is here. Who . . . ?' She turned to Melanie. 'Miss Marcia Dawson to speak with you.'

Melanie frowned as she took the telephone receiver.

'Hello, Marcia?'

'Melanie? So you're back in Barholme. I wondered if Miss Kendall would talk you out of it.'

'No,' said Melanie, evenly. 'I'm home for good now, Marcia.'

'Oh, surely not! Look, I'm in Manchester now, my dear. I decided to travel on to Manchester this morning and give myself a little more time here. I'm sorry we didn't have time for a proper talk, but I really do need your help, Melanie dear. I'm sorry I had to disillusion you over Carlton and Miss Kendall. They really do mean well, and they think they are doing their best for you, I'm quite sure, but they can't always see that plans which suit them do not always suit other people.'

'I'm really not very interested, Miss

Dawson,' said Melanie.

'You should be thanking me,' said Marcia, briskly. 'Don't you realize what I risked to save you from making a fool of yourself? I've known and loved Carlton for years, yet I deliberately risked his displeasure for you. I might have married him years ago but I wouldn't, because I know what he is. He's a wonderful person, but music will always come first with him. Can you understand that? All else must be sacrificed, if needs be, and you ought to be very grateful to me instead of sulking. Surely you must see what I mean. You're not a stupid girl, or I wouldn't be asking you to play for me.'

Melanie caught her breath, wanting to hang up the telephone, yet realising that Marcia Dawson had a point. Marcia *had* stuck her neck out, and she had certainly risked making the Kendalls very angry. And Carlton *did* put his heart into his music.

'Won't you be seeing Carlton again?' she asked Marcia.

'Of course I will, but not till he gets over his annoyance with me. Oh, he's been furious with me before now, but he'll get over it. He always does. But I wouldn't allow him to exploit a young girl like you. I know you won't feel like thanking me just yet and that you are finding it difficult to be grateful, but I'm not such an ogre, Melanie. I only sound like one. We've never really had a chance to get to know one another, we two. Miss Kendall was always very clever about seeing to that. Just think of the number of times she encouraged you to go out with Carl on your own. And if you remember that stomach upset which I had on board ship, I'm sure that she encouraged me to eat something which disagreed with me. Oh, I don't mean she put anything in my food! But she would keep offering me extra dishes, and I didn't want to seem boorish. Besides, she knew exactly what to give me to put me right again.'

'She couldn't know you would be upset by the food,' Melanie defended.

'I knew you wouldn't be grateful,' said Marcia with a sigh.

Melanie hardly knew what to say. Marcia was now giving her a completely new point of view.

'I am grateful,' she said at length.

'Good girl. Are you grateful enough to take up the job I offered you? Maybe I didn't tell you how I really felt about the way you played my accompaniments. Carlton kept saying that you just weren't good enough, and I didn't want to argue with him, but you seem to have a special feeling for accompaniments and we worked together very well. Willy is still in hospital, I'm afraid, and I do want this tour to be a success.'

'How long is the tour?' Melanie asked.

'Three weeks. Surely you can spare me three weeks of your time when I went out of my way to protect you. You'll know what I mean when you look back on it one day, but it will be too late by then.'

She was right, thought Melanie, with

resignation. She did owe Marcia something.

'What do you want me to do?' she asked.

'Catch the first available train for Manchester. I'm staying at the Midland, and I can book you a room. My first concert is on Saturday evening, but we must have rehearsals first of all. That's important. Please try to come straight away.'

'Could you wait a moment, please, Marcia?'

Melanie put down the receiver and ran to find Mrs. Price.

'Do you think you could carry on here for a few more weeks?' she asked. 'You and Shelley? I'm sorry if you had new plans made . . . we haven't had time to discuss them, have we? . . . but Miss Dawson would like me to play for her on tour.'

'Then of course you must help her,' said Mrs. Price. 'She appears to need you badly since she travelled here to look for you the other day.'

'We talked in Edinburgh,' said Melanie, briefly.

'That's okay then. We'll continue to do our best for you here, my dear, if you are satisfied with what we have done already.'

'Very satisfied,' Melanie agreed and hurried back to talk to Marcia.

It was only later, when she was on the train bound for Manchester that Melanie remembered the relief which Mrs. Price had shown when she told the older woman that she would be leaving again shortly. Was it because Mrs. Price was pleased that her job was safe for another week or two? Or was there some other reason? She had an uneasy feeling that the Prices were holding something back from her.

Melanie had to get used to a new Marcia Dawson. The girl did her best to fuss over her a little and to make her feel welcome when she arrived, but soon they were into the hard work of rehearsals, and Marcia's tantrums came to the fore. If Melanie's playing was less than perfect, she found that a great deal of wrath was being heaped on her head, and she spared a brief thought for William. How had he stood Marcia all these years?

At first she had minded very much indeed, and her own temper would begin to smoulder so that she answered back, rather promptly, when taken to task. She remembered that Carlton had accused Marcia of throwing tantrums when she was on tour, and now Melanie knew what he meant. But after a while they seemed to take the measure of one another, and to work together very well.

Marcia Dawson had a truly wonderful voice, thought Melanie, as they managed to get through the first performance faultlessly. It was then that she could see how the hard work and the meticulous attention to detail had paid off. Much should be forgiven Marcia because of her artistry.

'It's a privilege to work with you,' she

told Marcia, later, 'even if I don't find it easy at times.'

'You'll improve,' Marcia told her, sweetly.

It was the sort of remark which usually had the lights sparking out of Melanie's red hair, since a great many of the mistakes had been Marcia's when they were rehearsing, even though she would admit to none. But she was learning to hold her tongue, and she was also learning how to be an accomplished accompanist.

'I'm very glad the concert has been broadcast,' said Marcia, with satisfaction. 'I expect Carlton will ring to offer his congratulations.'

'If he does, please don't tell him I'm playing for you,' Melanie begged. 'I don't want to . . . to have any contact with him.'

'I don't have to tell him,' Marcia informed her. 'I'm sure he knows already. Your name will have been announced as my accompanist. I told you the work would be rewarding.'

'Oh dear,' said Melanie, her heart lurching. 'I . . . I didn't think of that.'

But Carlton did not ring, and when Marcia decided to get in touch with him, she found herself speaking to Mrs. McAndrew.

Melanie listened to a one-sided rather imperious-sounding conversation, then Marcia put down the telephone and turned to her.

'Neither Carl nor Miss Kendall are at home,' she said, turning to Melanie. 'That Mrs. McAndrew is a moron. I can't get a word of sense out of her.'

'I find her particularly intelligent,' said Melanie.

'Then she's deliberately obstructive, but I think she's telling me the truth when she says they are not at Ardlui. I'll try London.'

Fascinated in spite of herself, Melanie waited while Marcia rang every number where she was likely to locate Carl, starting with the hotel in Kensington.

'They've only just *had* a holiday,' she

said, crossly. 'He can't still be angry with me, and hiding from me. Where can he and Miss Kendall have gone? What about you? Have you any ideas?'

Melanie shook her head. Since leaving Ardlui she had felt a great emptiness in her heart. It was ironic that she might be enjoying this tour with Marcia very much, if only Carlton Kendall were still in her life. But now she was paying her debt of gratitude to Marcia for ensuring that she and Carl went their separate ways. But how much she missed him!

Melanie's days and nights became a vast round of rehearsals, scenes, control of temper, then joy and satisfaction. It must be invaluable to her in experience, yet she felt as though her life was suspended between the life she had known, and the future which was very dark. The tour was showing Melanie once again, that a life of teaching music in Barholme, and of taking responsibility for Jordan's, would be harrowing for her. Even if Mrs. Price consented to take on the job permanently, it would not solve all Melanie's own problems.

And always, too, there was this feeling of unease regarding the Prices. They were hiding something. She was sure of that now as she viewed her return home in retrospect. It had been heart-warming to be welcomed home so warmly, but behind it all she had detected an air of tension. Was that because of her violin? Had Miss Kendall made some sort of arrangement with Jane Price over that? Melanie shook her head. She was becoming obsessed with that violin, ever since Marcia had told her it may be valuable.

*　*　*

Towards the end of the tour, Melanie and Marcia relaxed one evening in the lounge of their hotel. Marcia was looking tired, but more relaxed and fulfilled than Melanie had ever seen her. She was beginning to understand the pattern of the other girl's life and to recognise that she lived mainly for her music. A great many things were minor irritations with which she dealt according to her mood in the ordinary course of events. If anyone angered her, she could be rude and inconsiderate, but as she settled down to give of her best, the real Marcia came through for a short time, and towards the end of each tour or concert, she was at her best, as a woman.

'Are you really in love with Carlton?' Melanie asked her, feeling that they now knew one another well enough for her to ask such a question.

Marcia was sitting back in her chair with her eyes closed. She had kicked off her shoes, and she looked relaxed and at ease with herself. For a moment she made no reply, then suddenly Melanie was startled to see two large tears rolling down her cheeks.

'Why . . . Marcia!' she cried. 'I'm so sorry. I should not have asked. It . . . it's none of my business . . . '

'No, it isn't,' said Marcia, with a

touch of her usual asperity, 'but I'll try to answer honestly. It's good for me to tell someone. I love Carlton as much as it is possible for me to love a man, but if you ask me whether I love Carlton more than I love my career, then I . . . I don't know. I just don't know. I would have to be passing both of them as I fell to my death, to know which one I would grab. Do you follow me?'

'I think so,' said Melanie.

Marcia searched in her handbag and brought out a tissue and quickly wiped her eyes.

'This is sheer easing of tension,' she said, briskly. 'I hope you understand that. I never cry, except at the end of a tour, or an important concert. And no one sees me crying. You understand?'

'Of course I do,' said Melanie, softly.

'Anyway . . . ' Marcia looked around, then she turned to look at Melanie again. 'I'd better tell you the rest of it. I ruined Carl's career, you know. Oh, I never meant to admit that to *any-one* . . . least of all you . . . or myself,

232

even. I was in a tantrum, as usual. We were doing a difficult television concert, and Carl was trying to make me relax. But as I say, I can't relax until it's all over. I'm sure you know what I mean.'

Melanie nodded. 'Yes, I know.'

'We'd had dinner, then we had a difference of opinion over something. I remember perfectly what it was, though it doesn't help to go into that with you. He was still sitting at the table, but I was walking up and down. I could feel myself tight inside with nerves. You don't have my sort of nerves, do you?'

'I do get nervous,' said Melanie, 'but . . .'

'Oh, this is different,' Marcia went on, impatiently. 'I believe one can get drugs for this sort of thing, to reduce the adrenalin, you know. Carl would not see my point of view, though I just knew that it would improve my performance enormously, and I thought he was being obstructive. I . . . I rushed at him with my hands outstretched, and I knocked over a candle just beside him. He was wearing his evening shirt, and the sleeve caught alight, and somehow everything I did from then on seemed to make things worse. He was in terrible pain and could hardly think for himself and there was no one nearby to help. I had searched for something to put out the flames, and . . . and I poured some wine on to his sleeve. That made it worse, but eventually we got the flames out, and I telephoned for the doctor. But it . . . it was horrible.'

'Oh dear,' said Melanie, her whole mind shrinking from the pain Carlton must have suffered.

'I begged him to forgive me,' Marcia went on, 'and I said it was an accident. He agreed that it was an accident, but I don't think he has ever really forgiven me. He had always loved me, but . . . but I have lost him. So now my choice is made. It must be my career, though if I must be honest, it taught me which I would choose if put to the test. It would have been Carlton every time. While he remains unattached, I cannot stay away from him. I must always go back.'

Melanie did not know what to say. She felt a deep sympathy for Marcia Dawson, and even more for Carlton who had suffered so much, emotionally as well as physically. Was he still torn in two between the love he had had for Marcia and resentment that through her actions his career was having to be reshaped?

Melanie thought again about the times she and Carlton had shared. For him it must have been like a holiday romance. She thought about Miss Kendall and how the older woman had encouraged this, but now she could see why. Miss Kendall must be incensed at Marcia for causing Carl's accident. She probably knew all about it, and hated Marcia for her part in it. She had encouraged Carl to turn to Melanie instead, but she could not break the ties which bound Carl and Marcia Dawson.

'Perhaps he will get over it if he makes a new career as a composer,' she said, gently, as the tears now slipped down Marcia's cheeks. 'Perhaps his music will bring him in a decent income again.'

'Oh, his income won't be at all bad,' Marcia said, wiping her eyes. 'No need to worry about him on *that* account. We both earn quite a lot from the recordings we made after that series of T.V. programmes . . . 'Fireside Music' . . . you know what I mean.'

'Indeed I do,' said Melanie slowly. 'I've seen several L.P's. But in that case . . . ' Her eyebrows wrinkled, ' . . . in that case, why did you say he was hoping to marry me because of my Amati violin? I mean, it isn't certain that I would get all that much money, if I *did* want to sell it. I might be able to follow your reasoning if . . . if Carlton were desperately hard up and willing to take an enormous gamble, but if he . . . if *both* of you collect royalties . . . '

Marcia's tears had dried, and she looked at Melanie then laughed a little. 'You *are* an innocent child, aren't you? All right, it was a bit far-fetched, and you fell for it, you silly girl. Not that it has made much difference to you, of course. You just cut your stay with the Kendalls rather short, that's all. But I needed someone to replace Willy, and I knew you could work with me. I could tell that on board ship, so you were my obvious choice. Besides,' ... Marcia leaned back and put her hands behind her head, ' ... your job with Carlton had been accomplished, and he'll be starting to use his arm soon again. When I anger him and he forgets himself, he can wave it about very well indeed. I had a word with Sloan, too, and Carl is going to see another specialist who is certain he can do something for him.'

'So you deliberately told me a lie,' said Melanie. She felt as though the breath had been knocked out of her body.

'Not at all. Dear Aunt Millicent told us about that violin of yours after your father died, and said that if the 'dear child' ever needed money badly, and did not set great personal store by it, then she would try to sell it for you. She was going to do you a favour, dear. She's a great do-gooder, isn't she?, always running around helping people. *She*'s the one who collects the 'lame ducks', you know. You . . . and the Prices . . . '

'Oh, how can you . . . ' cried Melanie.

'Well, the truth can't hurt now, can it?' asked Marcia, languidly. 'I needed you, and it's been quite a success, hasn't it? You've been very good, you really have. Not in Willy's class, I grant you, but as good as any I could have found, and that might have taken more time than I had to spare. I know you're angry now, darling, just like Carl is at times, but you'll soon simmer down and play for me again if Willy can't do it. Won't you?'

'No, I won't!' cried Melanie, furiously. She was so angry that tears were starting in her eyes. 'You made me look a complete fool in front of Miss Kendall and Carlton. Miss Kendall thought I *ought* to know what you were really like, but I didn't. I really didn't. The Kendalls were trying to help me, but I believed you, and I didn't even ask them if it was the truth. You . . . you're awful, Marcia. Do you know that? You are really awful.'

'I know,' said Marcia, calmly. 'But as I say, I needed you, and if you were fool enough to fall for it, then the more fool you. You've been well enough paid, haven't you? And you've gained in experience, and even a bit of publicity. What are you complaining about?'

Melanie ran a hand through her hair.

'But you stood to lose the Kendalls's respect for you as well, telling blatant lies like that. Didn't that worry you?'

'Oh, Carl knows me,' said Marcia, 'and so does Miss Kendall. They know I was testing you out . . . for them as well as myself. It was easy, wasn't it?'

'I . . . I'll never play for you again,' said Melanie, huskily. 'I'm so ashamed.

I'll never look Carl or . . . or Miss Kendall in the face again either.'

'Well, as I say, I've got Willy back from next week, you know. Did I mention that? And you'll never be a Willy, darling, though you are good. And really, you *were* getting a little bit involved with Carl, and if I have to lose him to another woman, I would prefer to lose him to someone with great talent and not a mediocre girl. He would soon grow bored with you, so I've done you both a favour. He's probably disgusted with you now.'

'And with you,' Melanie flashed, 'as I am. You've got the voice of an angel, but . . . but you're horrible. For a while I thought I was getting to know you, and even to like you a little, but all the time you were like this underneath.'

'I still give pleasure to millions. I don't have to be nice all the time. It gets wearing. I like to be as horrible as I want when I let off steam. It's like slipping out of a tight dress and putting on old slippers instead of those shoes

which were killing me. Carl under-
stands. So you needn't go trying to tell
him what a naughty girl I am. Deep
down he still loves me, even though he
knows me through and through.'

'I thought you said he was attracted
to Shelley Price. That was another lie, I
suppose.'

Marcia shrugged. 'I told you, pretty
girls always fall about over Carl. We
both love him though, don't we,
Melanie? I've watched you, and it's not
just a passing fancy. You love him, just
as I do, but I can live with it. You can't.
Go home and marry that salesman, or
whatever he is. Settle down and bring
up a family, and after a while you'll
forget Carl. That's more in your line,
really. Leave public life to Carl and me.'

'You have just been offering me a
new career as an accompanist.'

'I've changed my mind. You aren't
ruthless enough. You haven't the tem-
perament. You allow me to make
mincemeat out of you.'

'Well, that's all in the past,' said

Melanie, firmly. 'I've been a fool. I've never met anyone like you before, and I . . . I don't even think there *is* anyone like you. I don't think I ever want to see you again.'

'One more concert and you can go. You know, in a funny sort of way I would like you a lot, if it weren't for Carl. I find our small skirmishes quite stimulating.'

Melanie merely shook her head. It was all part of Marcia's complex nature that she had to quarrel with someone. And how wrong she had been about her! Neither Miss Kendall nor Carl would ever want to see her again, yet how sorry she was to have left them.

Through her anger and disappointment, she was also feeling strangely relieved. Carlton had not been using her after all, nor had Miss Kendall. She had arranged everything for Melanie's own sake.

'I'm going up to my room now,' she said, clearly, 'and I'll be catching the train in the morning, Marcia.'

'We still have one concert to do.'

'Not with me.'

'Oh, I expect Willy will do it. He's a lot better now and he's probably getting bored. All right, you can go in the morning.'

Melanie looked at Marcia who seemed to be completely relaxed and contented. Were all these so-called tantrums so necessary to her? How could one tell when she was telling the truth? Tomorrow she would probably deny everything.

Slowly she turned and made her way upstairs to her room.

12

Melanie travelled home by train, her thoughts going round and round. Marcia had seen her away, almost with affection, but Melanie felt she just did not want to know! Dare she write a note of apology to Miss Kendall? she wondered. Dare she even write to Carlton?

As she travelled on the last stage of her journey to Barholme, her thoughts went once again to Mrs. Price and Shelley. The decision to stay at home and teach, while keeping on Jordan's, had now been made for her. All along she had hoped that she might have a career on the concert platform, if not as a performer, then as an accompanist. Marcia had raised her hopes over that, but this experience with Marcia had put paid to that idea. Now she would have to make new arrangements with Mrs.

Price. It would be wonderful if the older woman could continue to run the business successfully, since she did it so well, and Melanie was sure she could pay Mrs. Price quite well now for her work.

But accommodation would be quite a problem. Would she be happy to share the flat indefinitely? Melanie bit her lip, feeling doubtful about such an arrangement. She was remembering Shelley's remark that she did not know how Melanie would feel about something. About what? Melanie knew she would have to resolve that question before any further arrangements could be made.

Once again she found a warm welcome waiting for her when she returned to the flat. She had telephoned that morning, and everything now was in readiness for her.

'We listened to some of the concerts on radio,' Mrs. Price said, her eyes shining happily. 'It was so nice to hear your name being mentioned.'

Melanie knew how much the older

woman loved music.

'I'm glad you enjoyed it,' she smiled.

'Marcia Dawson really has a marvellous voice.'

'Marvellous,' Melanie agreed, shortly. The other girl still set her teeth on edge, every time she remembered Marcia's conduct.

'Did you wear your gorgeous evening dresses?' asked Shelley.

'Only once or twice,' Melanie smiled in spite of herself. 'Sometimes I wore simpler gowns for afternoon concerts in library theatres.'

Shelley was really very young, and very appealing with her innocent beauty, and her eager interest in clothes and make-up.

'Has George returned home yet?' Melanie asked.

There was a short silence during which Mrs. Price arranged the tea table neatly and competently.

'Yes,' she said at length. 'He has been here until a short time ago, then he had to go to a meeting of the

Photographical Society. I expect you know how interested he is in Photography. But no doubt you will see him in the morning.'

Again Melanie detected a certain lack of ease, and she resolved to ask George what it was all about. If there had been trouble, then George would tell her so much more readily than Mrs. Price.

★ ★ ★

George Aldridge looked very well, and even more full of confidence than usual when Melanie saw him next day. She had decided to go next door to talk to Mr and Mrs. Aldridge, and she was enjoying a cup of coffee when George appeared.

'Melanie!' he greeted her, kissing her cheek. 'You look great. That holiday must have done you the world of good. Oh, and thank you so much for my gift. I was planning to come and see you later today to tell you how much I appreciated it.'

Melanie smiled. Mrs. Aldridge had just been telling her that she looked tired and had obviously been working too hard!

'So do you, George,' she said, looking at his glowing looks with interest.

Mr. and Mrs. Aldridge had made an excuse to leave them alone together.

'How have things been with you?' she asked. 'Did you manage to get on well with Mrs. Price and Shelley? They have made a wonderful difference to Jordan's, haven't they?'

'They're both splendid,' said George with enthusiasm, 'and . . . Melanie . . . I . . . I've rather fallen in love with Shelley. I feel I must be honest with you about that straight away. I know what we were to one another, but I'm sure that we were really more like brother and sister, weren't we? I've always loved you, just like a brother, you know.'

Melanie's mouth had fallen open with surprise, then she began to laugh. 'George!'

'I know that you probably think it is

very sudden,' he went on, earnestly, 'but it really hit me suddenly, Melanie. I'd never even seen a girl as lovely as Shelley before, and I truly didn't know what real love was like till I met her. Melanie, I'm sorry if I'm hurting you, but please try to understand.'

Melanie's eyes were brimming with laughter as she looked into George's anxious eyes.

'How does Shelley feel about you, George?'

'Oh, she's *very* much in love with me,' George assured her. 'We are hoping to be married soon. Father is going to retire, you know, and he and Mother have bought a cottage on the West Coast, at Girvan. Shelley and I plan to live here, and Mrs. Price . . .'

'Yes?'

'That's the only snag,' George admitted. 'She refuses to live with us. She says it is killing to a young couple to have mother-in-law in the next bedroom. Shelley and I have been rather worried, wondering what to do because Shelley doesn't want to leave her on her own.'

'Well, don't worry too much, George,' said Melanie. 'We'll see what can be done. Oh and congratulations! I know you will both be very happy.' A thought struck her. 'Oh, by the way, did you ever find out why Shelley wanted the key to my private cupboard?'

'Oh . . . that!' George shrugged. 'She couldn't find the cardboard boxes for packing things, and she thought they might be in that cupboard. Then I remembered that you had put those in the attic. We found them there without any trouble.'

'Thank you, George,' said Melanie, rather wearily. 'You know, I think we ought to have a celebration party. We certainly seem to have a great deal to celebrate. How about it?'

'Great!' said George. 'I will pop along to the jeweller's to see if Shelley's engagement ring is ready now. It's being engraved you know, with our initials inside entwined hearts, I thought.'

'Oh, I see . . . a lovely idea,' said Melanie.

'Yes, I thought so,' said George, pleased.

'You're happy, aren't you, George,' asked Melanie, softly, and the colour glowed in his face.

'Yes, I'm happy, Mel. I've never been so happy in my whole life.'

Melanie nodded. She had known such moments herself.

The atmosphere in Jordan's lightened considerably when Melanie went back to congratulate Shelley on her engagement.

'Then you don't mind?' the girl asked.

'Of course not. I'm delighted for you both. I . . . er . . . ' Melanie paused for a moment. 'I wondered for a little while how well you knew Mr. Kendall.'

'Oh, he's been like an uncle to me,' said Shelley, with affection, and Melanie blinked. Surely Carlton was not that old!

'Oh,' she said.

'Yes, I've written to tell him, and Miss Kendall, about my engagement to George and I'm hoping they will come over to wish us well at our party.'

'Well, that would be nice,' said Melanie, rather faintly. What would Carlton's reaction be when he saw her again?

'And you don't really mind?' asked Mrs. Price, gently. 'I've been so worried, Melanie dear. From what George said when we first arrived, I understood that you and he were . . . well . . . *very* special friends, and were even planning to marry one day after you had got over losing your father. Then after a while I could see that he and Shelley were attracted to one another. It has been rather a worry to me, as I pondered on what I could do. I thought it would be a sad home-coming for you to find that Shelley and George were engaged to be married, especially since you've only just lost your father, and you've been so kind to the two of us. It seemed so ungrateful somehow.'

'I'm delighted for them, Mrs. Price,' said Melanie, and the older woman could not doubt her sincerity.

'I shall advertise for pupils next week, and teach both piano and violin,' said Melanie, 'but I don't know what to do about the shop. Are you happy to be running it, Mrs. Price? I mean, you're fitted to run something much more . . . well . . . salubrious than Jordan's, aren't you?'

The older woman smiled. 'It's been wonderful for me, here, now that I'm on my own. I'm not under pressure here, and there has been time to get to know people, and to make friends. I'm older now and I find that Jordan's is as much of a challenge as I would wish. Besides, I feel I'm getting somewhere with this business. I don't know your plans, but please try to keep it all on the lines I'm laying down. I'm sure you will find that best.'

'I do wish you would consider staying on permanently, after Shelley marries

George. I think the flat would hold both of us, Mrs. Price, though I was uncertain about three. We could each have our own private room, and share facilities, and we could come to a good financial arrangement, I'm quite sure. If you ran Jordan's, I would teach, and we wouldn't get in one another's way.'

It looked as though the sun had come out, thought Melanie, as Jane Price turned to her. The older woman's face had lit up, and her eyes were glowing.

'Oh, my dear, I've been so uncertain about the future,' she said, huskily. 'I love it here, and I love the job . . . and Shelley would be so near. That really would be marvellous.'

'It's settled then,' said Melanie, and kissed the older woman's cheek.

How she wished she could settle down herself, and come to terms with her new life, thought Melanie a few days later. Shelley and Mrs. Price were planning a party for Friday evening, and several invitations had been sent out.

'You *will* play for us, won't you, Melanie?' she asked. 'I specially love to hear you play the violin and it's been lovely to hear you practising so much. You seem to get a beautiful tone out of the old instrument which belonged to your great-grandfather. Who made it, did you say?'

'I've been meaning to allow you to examine it,' said Melanie. 'I know you're interested, but I do tend to treat it carefully. It is very old and was made in Cremona, in Northern Italy, by Nicolaus Amati. I've always understood it was quite rare, but I've been told that it may be quite valuable now. I haven't tried to find out for certain since I don't wish to sell it.'

'What makes it so valuable?' asked Shelley. 'Its age?'

'Oh well, darling, they did have the secret of violin-making in Cremona,' said her mother. 'The Stradivarius and Guarnerius both came from there. The violins are beautifully made from finest wood, and I've heard it said that the secret lay in the varnish which was used.'

'That's probably correct,' said Melanie. 'My father set great store by that when he finished off his violins.'

She put down the old violin lovingly, and picked up the one her father had made.

'He managed to produce these violins, and you can hardly tell the difference in tune unless you listen very carefully.'

She played a few bars of melody.

'He made the bass bar, here, rather longer and he has raised the bridge and increased the curve, but only a fraction really.'

'It certainly produces a wonderful tone,' Mrs. Price remarked.

'It has eighty-four pieces,' said Melanie, 'all different.'

The telephone shrilled, and shortly afterwards the doorbell and both Mrs. Price and Shelley ran off to answer them. Melanie was left on her own as she tuned and tested each of her precious violins. They needed constant care, and she was working on both of them, after having left them behind for safe keeping when she went to Greece. She also had to catch up on the hours of practice she liked to put in each day.

On impulse she picked up the Amati and began to play part of the lovely music which Carlton had written, inspired by the Greek Islands. Part of it would not come right, and she knew it was not as she remembered it, but was unsure how to put it right. Softly she began to play the slow movement again, and the tears tightened in her throat. How beautiful it was, and how close it brought Carlton. But again she hesitated over the difficult passage.

''A flat', not 'sharp',' said a voice behind her and she whirled round, her heart leaping with shock.

'Carl!, she gasped. 'You! I . . . I was only . . .'

'I know. I was listening. You play the violin like an angel, Melanie. Why didn't you tell me? Your piano is

257

competent, but fairly ordinary apart from accompaniments, but your violin . . . that's different. That violin you're holding is in the hands of a young master.'

Melanie was trembling so much that she could hardly take in what he was trying to say.

'Oh, Carl, I'm so sorry,' she whispered. 'I listened to Marcia Dawson's lies. I didn't even ask you if she was telling the truth. I'm so ashamed.'

'Oh, that!' said Carl. 'That's all over, and wasn't in the least important. I was very angry at the time, but I know Marcia and she always makes me angry. But I've learned to take all she has to tell me with a pinch of salt, and I knew you would find her out sooner or later. No, my dear, I have been avoiding you. I admit it. But I felt I couldn't ask you to share my life until I knew that my arm was going to be no serious handicap to me. You're so young, you see, and you've got all your life before you. You couldn't be tied down to an old crock like me.'

'Old crock! Never that, Carl.'

'No? I felt like an old crock at times. You see, I fell in love with you but I couldn't ask you to marry me until I saw the specialist again. I had to have hope.'

'To *marry* you!' she said.

He came to draw her into his arms, his own arm no longer quite so stiff, but far from perfect.

'Yes, I think I began to love you from the first, darling. Your red hair makes you rather noticeable, my sweet, and you do keep flying off the handle.'

'I'm going to fly off the handle now,' cried Melanie. 'You say you . . . you loved me from the first yet you let me walk out of your life and . . . and be miserable while you go off and see if anything can be done about your arm, which is completely unimportant to me. What do *I* care about whether you are disabled or not, when I love you as you are.'

Carlton bent to kiss her.

'Stop yelling,' he said, gently. 'You're beginning to sound like Marcia.'

'But I might have . . . have married someone else, on the rebound or something.'

'Would you?' He grinned at her. 'I don't think so. Did you think I would let you go so easily? I was keeping an eye on you, and I would never have let you go until I was sure you would be happier without me, than with me.'

'I could never have been happy . . . truly happy . . . without you, Carl,' said Melanie. 'I've been so miserable over this past few weeks.'

'Oh, darling, I am sorry,' he told her, tenderly. 'You see, I've been having intensive treatment to try to improve the general condition, and I do wish I could tell you that it is quite better, but you see, Melanie, it will never be really better again. I can use it a little, but that's all.'

'As if that mattered!'

'Melanie, you have never seen my arm unbandaged, but the bandages are off now. It isn't a pretty sight, though the appearance can be helped in time. I think you had better look before you finally decide that you are going to marry me.'

Melanie stood quite still while Carl slipped off his jacket, then rolled up the sleeve of his shirt. The arm was scarred and puckered, and the tissue badly discoloured. Melanie's heart was wrung when she thought of what he must have suffered.

'Oh, Carl,' she whispered, then saw the familiar withdrawn look in his eyes as his lips tightened. Suddenly she was able to understand his moods so well.

'Stop looking like that!' she cried. 'I won't have it. You really have made me miserable, thinking that you've had to go through all this pain. Marcia told me all about it, and this time I think she told me the truth, and it hurt, Carl. It really hurt. But if you think that a scarred arm is likely to stop me loving you, then you are very much mistaken. What kind of girl do you think I am?'

She watched the shadows vanishing as he rolled his sleeve down again, and came to take her in his arms, and suddenly they were laughing together for sheer joy.

'You're a wonderful girl,' he told her. 'I think I knew from the start that I wouldn't allow anyone else to have you.'

'I'm so happy,' said Melanie. 'Oh, Carl, I never thought I could be so happy. What about Miss Kendall? Has she forgiven me yet for walking out on you both?'

'Of course,' said Carl. 'She's a very sensible woman is my Aunt Millicent, and she knows what is best for everyone. Haven't you noticed that? She could see straight away that you and I were meant for one another. I've got strict instructions to bring you home to Ardlui, even for a short while, and allow her and Mrs. McAndrew to fuss over you a little. I expect we'll have to arrange a wedding fairly soon and put them out of their misery.'

'What a reason for getting married!' said Melanie, teasingly.

Carlton's eyes suddenly fell on her violin.

'Is this the famous instrument?' he asked. 'In a moment I would like to hear you playing it again. Darling, I think, perhaps, I could write my music for you to interpret. I could do it through you, if you were willing to be my . . . my . . . '

'Arm?' she asked.

'Other self,' he said, gently. 'I've got a dear friend, another well-known conductor who likes my 'Enchanted Island'. Melanie, if we work very hard together, do you think you could play it for me? It is going to be included in a special performance at the next Gala Performance on television. I must warn you, though, that Marcia will be singing on the same show, but I think you will find that her attitude towards you will be quite different when she realizes that you can really play that violin. She always admires the artiste.'

'Oh, Carl!' cried Melanie, her face going white with nerves at the thought. Then she faced him honestly.

'Why not, my darling? It's wonderful music and I feel that part of it belongs to me already. I can put my heart into it, and don't worry about Marcia. I think I really know her at last.'

'Thank you, darling,' said Carlton Kendall, simply. 'Thank you for my life.'

THE END

We do hope that you have enjoyed reading this large print book.

Did you know that all of our titles are available for purchase?

We publish a wide range of high quality large print books including:
Romances, Mysteries, Classics
General Fiction
Non Fiction and Westerns

Special interest titles available in large print are:
The Little Oxford Dictionary
Music Book, Song Book
Hymn Book, Service Book

Also available from us courtesy of Oxford University Press:
Young Readers' Dictionary
(large print edition)
Young Readers' Thesaurus
(large print edition)

For further information or a free brochure, please contact us at:
Ulverscroft Large Print Books Ltd.,
The Green, Bradgate Road, Anstey,
Leicester, LE7 7FU, England.
Tel: (00 44) 0116 236 4325
Fax: (00 44) 0116 234 0205